HOGAN JACKED A ROUND INTO THE CAR-15's CHAMBER

Cursing himself for not being more alert, he crawled along the ground toward the hill from where the shots came. Suddenly he heard the distinct sounds of broken branches cracking under somebody's weight.

One or more of the bandits must have managed to sneak behind him. He rolled sideways and twisted his body around, his finger ready on the trigger. Then there was a faint swishing, and the air seemed to acquire a luminous quality.

He was shaking his head, trying to clear his vision, when a towering figure appeared out of nowhere, clenching a huge broadsword in his hands.

The Guardian Strikes

WARRIORS TIME

David North

A GOLD EAGLE BOOK FROM
WORLDWIDE.

TORONTO · NEW YORK · LONDON · PARIS
AMSTERDAM · STOCKHOLM · HAMBURG
ATHENS · MILAN · TOKYO · SYDNEY

To the six not-usually patient Norths who suffered through the creation of this series without too many complaints.

First edition December 1991

ISBN 0-373-63603-2

THE GUARDIAN STRIKES

Copyright © by David North.
Philippine copyright 1991. Australian copyright 1991.

Printed in U.S.A.

The Guardian Strikes

PROLOGUE

Nis glanced out of his window at the huge metal-framed hemisphere covering the community. In it was everything needed to sustain life—ventilation systems, climate control devices, hydroponically grown crops and even a source of artificial sunlight.

Everything was going according to schedule, and there would be more than enough time to eliminate any opposition to his search.

As he studied the glass container that housed a small colony of ants, a lock of his yellow hair obscured his almond-shaped eyes for a moment. But that didn't bother him, and a look of satisfaction spread across his flawless features.

"How like the creatures that inhabit this world," he told himself as he saw the scurrying insects. "Always rushing back and forth."

He thought of the inhabitants of the thousands of worlds he had visited. All useless, like the planets on which they had lived, except for the few that had contained some quantities of the energy matter he sought.

This was one of the two remaining source planets. The other was in a different dimension. There was ample indication that a vast supply of the energy source was available on the two worlds.

Twice before, he had launched campaigns against the pair of planets, only to be thwarted by a pair of warlike creatures called Hogan and Brom.

Each time, he had abandoned his attempts at conquest to search other worlds, but none of them showed any evidence of the glowing stones.

Now he had returned with a new determination to survive.

He recognized where he had erred in the past.

This time he had acquired enough of the vital glowing rocks he needed to have the time to plan more carefully, and he had found ways to motivate followers on both planets.

On the more primitive of the two worlds he had recruited a power-hungry king, and on the more developed one he had taken advantage of a man's fanatic devotion to a popular cause among many of its inhabitants: *saving the planet from environmental destruction.*

Again Nis looked through the large window of his apartment unit inside the dome that covered the newly constructed city. It had been designed to be totally self-contained—to withstand any disaster short of a cataclysmic earthquake.

Beyond the reinforced glass of the curved panels that separated the colony from the outside world was the Australian outback.

It was a harsh, lifeless world outside the domed community, except for a handful of natives, reptiles and small animals.

A suitable model for how the rest of this world would soon become, Nis thought as he turned his attention back to the ant colony. Sitting near it was an aerosol can. Slipping off the top, he placed the nozzle of the container next to the opening that led to the network of tunnels.

Then he held the button down and watched the compressed-air-driven chemical force its way through the passageways.

One by one the insects ceased their movement, until at last the entire colony was dead.

1

"You drive like an old woman carrying a thousand eggs to market," Mok Seng remarked as he adjusted his saffron-colored robes.

He had been griping about their progress along the unpaved road since they had left the Angkor Wat ruins. He turned his head sideways and fixed his chauffeur with a stern glance.

"If you continue to move like a turtle, the man who is making my new glasses will be too old to fit them on me by the time we get to Battambang."

The regional capital was approximately one hundred and fifty miles southeast of the Buddhist temple that Mok Seng and Black Jack Hogan called home. Four hours by car on the potholed roads connecting the two places. And recently the site of several bandit attacks on innocent travelers.

But that didn't worry Hogan. He intimidated most people when they first saw him. He was built like a heavyweight boxer who looked ready and willing to fight a championship bout at the drop of a challenge. His hair was long, straight and dark blond, and hung down to his shoulders. His eyes were a disturbingly translucent blue. And his tall frame easily carried his two hundred and thirty pounds of well-trained muscle.

Black Jack, who had acquired the nickname because of his knockout record on his college boxing team, had volunteered to drive the Buddhist abbot to pick up the glasses he had ordered.

"Just another two hours, little grandfather," he said calmly. "We'll even have time to do some window-shopping before we have to drive back to the temple."

Though "little grandfather" was the literal translation for the Cambodian word for "Buddhist abbot," Hogan knew that Mok Seng didn't appreciate the constant reminder of his age. It was a fine way to needle him just a little bit when he got grumpy.

"After these many years of my trying to beat culture into you, you are still a *pnong*."

Pnong meant "barbarian," and it was Mok Seng's favorite insult whenever he was irritated at something Black Jack had done—or not done.

"You are also a poor student and a disrespectful son," he added in an aggrieved voice.

Son?

The American was surprised. He had lived at the temple as a lay person off and on for many years now. Each day he faced lessons in Buddhist philosophy, meditation and the art of self-defense as practiced for more than a thousand years by Buddhist clerics.

For a long time he had believed that the relationship between the Cambodian and himself was guest and host or teacher and occasional student.

All that had changed two years ago when the group of orphans he was escorting to a newly built orphanage was ambushed by a large band of Khmer Rouge Communist guerrillas armed with automatic weapons.

Left for dead, he found himself suspended in a series of strange nightmares. The devil refused him admission to hell. Then he fought battles alongside a strange red-bearded warrior who treated him like a god.

When he finally awakened from the coma, he was back in the Buddhist temple being tended by Mok Seng and his monks.

He remembered thanking his mentor for restoring him to life.

But the abbot's mournful reply had been less than enthusiastic.

"I shall regret what I have done. It is said that when one saves a life, one must take the responsibility for making that life better. In your case that will take a great deal of time and patience."

Though Mok Seng hadn't put his feelings in complimentary words, this was the first time he had acknowledged how he felt about Hogan.

"And I am not interested in the material things the world outside has to offer, so there will be no window-shopping," he said contemptuously.

Hogan understood the retreat from emotion. Like himself, Mok Seng had difficulty revealing affection.

"Not even for a new television set so you can watch kick-boxing matches?"

For a brief moment the Cambodian's eyes glistened. Then just as quickly became cold.

"To listen to them on the shortwave radio is enough. If one can see with his mind, one does not need a machine to show him pictures."

The man behind the wheel of the vintage Jeep smiled. He suspected Mok Seng was fully aware that he had ordered a television set be shipped to Battambang as a gift for the abbot, but needed to maintain his air of disdain as proof he had rejected the instruments of the world outside the temple.

Hogan thought it likely that Mok Seng was afraid of returning to civilization—even for a few brief hours—after spending most of his life in the temple tucked among the ruins of the ancient city of Angkor Wat.

He could appreciate such a reaction. Every time he left the calm environment of the temple to undertake another mission for the American government, Black Jack felt uncomfortable about returning to the world he had rejected so many years ago.

"It has been a long time since the man from Washington has called on you to travel," Mok Seng commented, interrupting his memories.

Mok Seng was right. It had been almost three months since Hiram Wilson had given him an assignment. Maybe the world was in better shape than he believed possible.

No way! he corrected himself immediately. From the few news reports he managed to hear on the shortwave radio, people were still busy trying to destroy each other—or the planet.

Problems like pollution and acid rain had not yet reached Cambodia. But he had no doubt they would not ignore his home for very long.

Home? Hogan smiled at the word.

He never intended to settle here. He'd come back to Cambodia ten years before as a counterinsurgency specialist on a secret mission for his government.

Then fate and lead from Cambodian guerrilla assault rifles kept him here until he was well enough to return to his own country.

Later he had nearly forgotten about the temple and its monks until he had to find a refuge quickly and could think of no other place to go.

He had come as an outcast from civilization, with no immediate family or friends, unless he counted Hiram Wilson, the Southerner who functioned as an Intelligence aide in the White House, as a friend.

Hogan didn't.

Mok Seng had made him spend three hours of each day exercising, gaining mastery over the complex wisdom of Gautama Siddhartha, who became known to his followers as Buddha, the intricacies of kung fu, the delicate movements of t'ai chi, the spiritual arts of the sword, the bow and the dueling sticks. Day after day he had repeated the drills, then had new ones added to them until even the dangerous missions Wilson sent him on seemed undemanding by comparison.

"We shall pass the time by reviewing a lesson," Mok Seng announced suddenly.

Black Jack groaned. He had looked forward to the journey by Jeep as an escape from his lessons.

"We shall discuss the Four Noble Truths of Buddha."

There was no point protesting. Hogan kept his eyes on the unpaved road ahead of him as he answered.

"Existence inevitably leads to unhappiness."

The small abbot grunted, "Good. At least you know what every schoolboy of six knows. What is the second Noble Truth?"

"Unhappiness is caused by desire," the American repeated in a monotone.

Mok Seng lightly punched Hogan's well-developed biceps. "Show interest, *pnong*. I am trying to force culture into your resisting mind. What is the third Noble Truth?"

Hogan's arm muscles ached from the seemingly light blow. Despite his age and size, the Buddhist monk was a powerful combatant, as the American knew well from his practice sessions.

"Unhappiness can be avoided by the crushing of desire," he mumbled.

Mok Seng punched the thick arm again.

"Hey, that hurts," Black Jack complained.

"Then show interest and learn how to rise above the pain. What is the fourth Noble Truth?"

Hogan tried to quickly to recall. Mok Seng would just continue tenderizing his muscles with blows until he answered.

With forced enthusiasm, the American began to reply, "Desire can be crushed by following the moral path that leads to—"

Just then, like a particularly heavy hailstorm, a barrage of .223 lead riddled the hood of the Jeep.

2

Hogan looked around quickly for cover as another barrage fractured the glass of the front windshield.

The attack was coming from the top of a small rise across the road. He stamped on the gas pedal and ran the Jeep into the thick foliage at the base of the hill.

After jamming on the brakes, with one hand he grabbed the gun belt that held a 9 mm 92-F Beretta automatic and a scabbard housing an ornate-handled eighteen-inch-long knife in one hand. Then, from the floor he scooped up the CAR-15 that was his constant companion.

"Get under cover," he yelled, then glanced at his companion. Mok Seng was slumped forward.

Suddenly worried, Hogan started to shake him, then saw the long bleeding groove along his right temple. He leaned his head against the other's chest and grabbed his wrist to feel for the pulse.

The abbot was alive, knocked out by the force of the slug that had creased the side of his head.

He dragged Mok Seng from the Jeep, pulled him to a thick stand of trees and vines and carefully lowered him to the ground.

"Stay alive, little grandfather, while I take care of this," he muttered as he strapped the gun belt around his waist and released the safety on the Beretta. Jacking a round into the CAR-15's chamber, Hogan patted the still form, then started his move against the hidden gunmen.

Cursing himself for not being more alert, he crawled along the ground toward the hill from where the shots came.

As he inched slowly up the hill, Hogan resumed the hunter posture of a trained jungle fighter. This would be the last attempted robbery for the hidden bandits, who were probably former Communist Khmer Rouge guerrillas. Generally they preferred to kill travelers rather than just rob them.

Suddenly he heard the distinct sounds of broken branches cracking under somebody's weight.

One or more of the bandits must have managed to sneak behind him.

He rolled sideways and twisted his body around, his finger ready on the trigger. Then there was a faint swishing, and the air seemed to acquire a luminous quality. He shook his head, trying to clear his vision when a towering figure appeared out of nowhere. It was Brom with his flaming beard, clenching a huge broadsword in his hands.

Brom had again responded to the connection they had between them, a connection they had somehow acquired when both of them were at death's door and that spanned time and space. Brom was from another world, and it was a mystery Hogan had no answers for.

Brom, who hailed from a warrior culture, was a massive collection of hardened muscles and sinew. His long, electric-red hair flowed down to his shoulders and matched the color of his rich full beard. His fearsome head was enough to strike terror in any opponent.

The huge, scalpel-sharp broadsword he carried in one hand was over thirty inches long and weighed close to forty pounds. Slung over a shoulder was an AK-47, and suspended from a belt around his waist was a krall—a long knife with an ornate hilt similar to the one he had given Hogan.

"I saw the tiny wise man lying still on the ground," Brom said. "Is he . . . ?"

Brom and Mok Seng knew of each other's existence, and had seen proof in several brief encounters in the past.

"No. Just injured. A group of bandits hiding someplace up on the hill ambushed us."

"Does peace ever exist in your world?"

"Not lately," the American admitted.

Brom shook his head, then started to charge ahead.

"Wait," Hogan called after him urgently.

The sword-wielding fighter halted, then turned to look at Black Jack with a puzzled expression.

"Wait for what, Hogan?"

Hogan knew that Brom preferred fighting to planning. As ruler of a country named Kalabria, he left the tedious political and business aspects in the hands of his most trusted adviser and counselor, the wise man known as Mondlock the Knower.

"Let's work out a strategy."

"We charge these savages and kill them. That is our strategy," the Kalabrian replied, and turned to resume his climb up the hill.

"No. We don't know how many of them there are. They're probably searching for Mok Seng and me right now."

"So we will find them before they find you."

Black Jack thought quickly. "Work your way around to the other side of the hill, then fire a couple of shots from your rifle into the air. That'll get their attention while I climb the hill and hit them from behind."

The Kalabrian shook his head. "That is not a good idea, Hogan."

"Why not?"

"The fire-stick is out of poison pellets."

Hogan sighed. Although Brom had learned to fire the weapon Hogan had given him as a gift, he still couldn't comprehend that once he had fired a round, he couldn't re-use it.

"Okay, we'll switch places," he decided. "But wait until you hear my shots before you attack."

At last they had agreement, and they separated.

The American worked his way through the tall broom grass and stands of bamboo. He deliberately stamped on the thick carpeting of fallen branches with his heavy black boots to attract the attention of the hidden assassins.

Tilting his CAR-15 skyward, he set the weapon on single shot and fired two rounds.

Right away terrified screams filled the air.

Brom had already reached the top.

As Hogan raced to the plateau, he saw the wicked glint of Brom's "howling" sword as it descended toward one of five stunned men clad in black pajamalike garments.

Their AK-47s of Chinese manufacture were momentarily forgotten at their astonishment at seeing the red-bearded figure come charging at them with an immense sword.

The razor-sharp edge of the blade sliced through the stomach of the gunman Brom had singled out, followed by a thin red gash that contrasted against his black clothes. Then there was a profuse stream of blood flowing to the ground, and before he even had time to respond, the man fell facedown into his own blood.

Recovering from their shock, the other four turned their automatic weapons on the Kalabrian.

Racing forward, Black Jack switched his weapon to full and emptied his clip with a sweeping motion.

One of them caught several bullets. Yelling in pain and anger, the gunman tried to fire his weapon as he fell and found his fingers wouldn't obey his brain's orders. But he wasn't dead yet.

Another man, bleeding from a wound, spun around and started to squeeze the trigger of his rifle when he had Hogan in his sights.

Then he looked on in horror as his arm holding the stock of the weapon to his shoulder was severed by a single blow from Brom's sword. His arm fell to the ground, and he collapsed after it as if he were trying to retrieve the severed limb.

Brom glanced at the blood that covered his blade as he turned away from the disabled assailant.

The man who had been felled by Hogan made a last desperate attempt, and hot lead whistled past Hogan, making him jump sideways.

Dropping his CAR-15, he whipped the Beretta from its holster and snap-aimed as he pulled back on the trigger.

The lead tore through the assassin's body with a final deadly message. But beside him, the one-armed man was getting ready to send his knife sailing through the air at Hogan.

Brom's heavy blade descended again, and the last adversary succumbed to the blow that nearly split his head.

Brom pulled his sword from the quivering form, then knelt down and wiped his blade on the green grass.

Holstering the Beretta, Hogan glanced at him. Brom's coarse white shirt and long wide pants were covered with bloodstains. But that didn't satisfy the fierce warrior.

He finished cleaning his sword, then stuck two fingers into one of the pools of blood.

Standing up, he ran his blood-covered fingers across his left and right cheeks.

Black Jack turned away. He understood that in Brom's world, a warrior painted the blood of the enemy he had slain on his face so that he could display his bravery before his gods after a battle. But every time he witnessed it, Black Jack found the practice repulsive.

Brom stood and grinned at him. "Will you paint yourself, Hogan?"

The American knew when he was being goaded. "What I don't need is more blood on me. What I *do* need is a bath—after I get Mok Seng to a doctor."

Through narrowed eyes, Brom studied the American. "You are looking fit, Hogan." He saw the knife at Hogan's waist. "I see you still carry the krall I gave you."

Taking it out of its scabbard, Hogan studied the ornate handle of the long knife. "I never go out without it. It impresses women."

"There is a former temple maiden who would not be pleased with that news," Brom commented with a grin. "She keeps wondering how you entertain yourself when you are away from her. How shall I answer her question?"

"Is Astrah still training as a dance warrior with your Mora?"

Mora was Brom's consort and the leader of an elite group of athletic young women skilled in acrobatics and the use of weapons.

Created by one of Brom's ancestors during a massive invasion of their land, the dance warriors were capable of serving alongside men when there was a desperate need for additional arms. For centuries, however, the group had been ceremonial, performing their daring feats at festivals and important public functions.

"Astrah has learned so fast that Mora has appointed her second in command of the dance warriors."

Hogan thought of the slight girl with hair the color of wild strawberries who had so quickly changed from a subservient temple maiden assisting the Kalabrian priests in their religious ceremonies to a strong, self-confident—and possessive—woman.

"Tell Astrah that I think of her whenever I'm not too busy trying to stay alive," Hogan said.

"For your sake I hope she believes me," the Kalabrian ruler replied, smiling.

A shimmering cloud was beginning to fill the air around them.

"Come to us soon, Hogan," Brom said as he moved to the glowing mist.

"All you have to do is get in trouble," Hogan cracked as he started to slip his krall back into its scabbard.

Then he saw a black form emerge from the forest and aim an AK-47 at Brom's back.

There was no time for warning. Hogan quickly balanced the long knife in his palm, then gripped the edge of the blade and threw it at the armed intruder.

The knife whistled through the air, then the carefully honed tip dug a path through the assassin's left thigh. The gunman, his face distorted with pain, grabbed at the blade and tried to pull it out.

Black Jack raced forward and threw himself at the other man.

Despite his wounds, the guerrilla fought with surprising strength and speed. He tried to chop at Hogan's carotid artery with the callused edge of his hand.

Swiftly leaning to one side, Hogan slashed down on the forearm of the attacker with his opened palm and, at the same time, threw a kick at the other's throat.

Expertly avoiding the move with a quick shuffling step, the dark-skinned guerrilla turned the freed blade on the American.

Black Jack kept dodging out of the way of the slashing knife, then waited for the small man to make his next move.

Slashing the air as he moved around Hogan, he snarled out in heavily accented English, "Now you will feel the vengeance of the people, pig!"

Hogan could hear Brom moving to his side. "No, he's mine," he called out, and Brom's footsteps retreated.

Beckoning to the guerrilla, Hogan issued a challenge and an insult. "Come and get me if you aren't built like a woman under your pajamas."

Anger flared in the man's bloodshot eyes. "You will be the one without a man's tools soon," he snapped back.

Hogan kept prodding the other with insults. "I wish your mother could be here and see the coward she raised."

"I send her your testicles as a birthday gift," the Asian hissed. Then after a feint to the left, he raised Hogan's krall and charged at him.

Black Jack waited until the man was almost upon him, then twisted aside and wrapped his arms around the other's head.

Reaching back with the knife, the smaller man wildly tried to reach flesh and bone.

For a moment Hogan was tempted to wrestle the man to the ground and wrest the blade from him, but he remembered that this wasn't a contest but a fight to live.

Slowly he squeezed his arms tighter, then deliberately twisted his opponent's neck with all the force he could gather.

There was the sound of bones cracking, and blood began to ooze out of the guerrilla's ears. Black Jack twisted again to make sure the trained killer was dead, then let the body drop to the ground.

As he reached down to pick up his krall, he noticed a large folded piece of paper that had to have fallen from the dead assassin's pocket.

Hogan picked it up, along with the AK-47 the gunman had carried. He started to head toward the thick vegetation to make sure there were no more hidden killers when he saw Brom standing between him and the woods. The Kalabrian was holding four of the automatic weapons that the dead attackers had used.

"These fire-sticks all have poison pellets in them," he explained, waving the guns. Then he added, "I checked the forests. There was no one else nearby."

Black Jack nodded approvingly. He had been careless not to check himself. Turning his attention to his find, he opened the piece of paper.

It was a detailed road map of Vietnam, Thailand, Laos and Cambodia. A circular route had been drawn in crayon from the southern Vietnamese village of Buon Me Thuot across Cambodia to Battambang. Then the crayoned route went north to Angkor Wat, from where it continued into Thailand and north to Chiang Rai in the upland hill country where independence-minded mountain tribes lived in armed truce with the Bangkok government.

Hogan looked back at the motionless bodies.

The attackers were not Khmer Rouge Cambodians as he had first suspected. Their features were too slim and pointed. They were Vietnamese. And they had been tracking him, probably hiring local spies for information of his movements.

But why? he wondered. He hadn't been on a mission for months. Or were they getting revenge for some action in the past?

Another puzzle was why Chiang Rai was marked on the map.

Black Jack hadn't been in the region since the war, when he used the hill country as a secret training ground for his counterinsurgency team.

But searching for answers would have to wait until after he got Mok Seng to a doctor.

Then he realized that the Kalabrian was still there.

"Stay alive, Hogan," Brom said, clasping forearms with the American. "I will be angered if you get yourself killed."

He moved to the glowing cloud that waited patiently across the thick, grassy field and stepped inside it.

"And so will the temple maiden," he added as the glowing haze swirled thickly around him.

"I'd hate to have her mad at me," Hogan shouted. And lose the familiar sweet fragrance of her delicate body next to me, he added to himself.

Then he sprinted downhill to attend to the unconscious Mok Seng.

3

The general grabbed the extended hand and shook it vigorously.

"We were honored that you came and visited us, Mr. Kalidonian. Their magesties wanted me to convey their personal gratitude for your efforts to save the Earth," he hissed politely.

Indeed, it was General Thant who—when he had received word that Argun Kalidonian was planning to tour the northern hills of Thailand—warned the other members of the royal cabinet that a visit from one of the richest men in the world was not an event the Thai government could ignore.

Even though he had disposed of his vast industrial holdings to devote the rest of his life to saving the environment, Argun Kalidonian was still a powerful man.

He was at the helm of the prestigious International Council on the Environment, and he had recruited experts on the subject to assist in preparing recommendations on saving the Earth and its natural treasures.

The story of how he had discarded the role of international industrialist to embrace the one of environmental activist had been publicized too often to still be a mystery.

The deaths of thousands of men, women and children caused by an explosion in a Kalidonian-owned fertilizer plant in India had received worldwide coverage. The fact that his only son, Raphael—general manager of the facility—and his son's wife and child were among the dead had also been widely reported.

Shortly after the massive tragedy, the elderly billionaire began to dispose of his holdings and dedicate himself to a variety of environmental causes. What had really touched Kalidonian was his personal loss. He was one of those people who aren't really moved by the destruction of others, but anything to do with him personally assumed tremendous importance.

As he had been in the world of business, Argun Kalidonian became a powerful influence among protest groups trying to save the forests, endangered species, the atmosphere—and the Earth itself.

His influence didn't extend to most of the leaders of the many nations in the world. Although Kalidonian and his fellow council members were publicly applauded for their efforts, their suggestions had been largely ignored by most of the United Nations members during their four years of existence.

General Thant was tempted to ask the visitor about the rumors that he had become so frustrated with the resistance his group had met that he was building an enclosed, self-contained community somewhere in Australia to which he planned to retreat. Protocol prevailed, and he refrained from asking the question. Instead, he opened a parchment scroll and read aloud from it.

"The royal government and people of Thailand pledge their cooperation in the work of the International Council on the Environment...."

"Yes, yes," Argun Kalidonian interrupted impatiently. "You can tell them I will personally praise their work at the next session of the council." He glanced at the others in his party who were boarding the custom-fitted Bell AH-1S helicopter. "Now we must leave. They are waiting for us in Vientiane."

"Ah, yes," the senior officer muttered disdainfully. "Laos. Perhaps you can convince the Laotian government to start cleaning up the mess they've made of their land."

Then they finished their goodbyes, and Kalidonian was soon ensconced in the helicopter's seat. As the pilot, one of Kalidonian's recruits, flew the helicopter north, the retired industrialist studied the jungle-speckled landscape below.

His expression was dispassionate, but inside he was seething with anger. As hard as he had tried, he knew he had failed to convince the world that they were on the edge of an environmental cataclysm. Dedicated environmentalists had joined him in trying to pressure their governments to turn the recommendations into law. But even they found themselves powerless to do anything but protest publicly.

Only the activist members of the environmental groups did more than complain. But despite their frequent terrorist acts against any who refused to cooperate, they too had found themselves powerless to make significant changes in the laws of their countries.

That was also the case with the other three passengers who had joined him in his campaign.

He was going to save the planet at any cost. He hoped he would not have to take drastic measures, but where logic and pleading hadn't worked, perhaps fear and terror would. If that failed, he was prepared to take the ultimate step.

What was needed was the right means, and one of the three aboard the helicopter, Marco Gussman, had found it through his contacts. But the price was high. When Kalidonian expressed his shock at a fee of thirty million dollars, Dr. Alexander Nis, his scientific adviser, indicated that the amount wasn't exorbitant considering that it had cost the United States government several billion dollars to develop it.

Kalidonian trusted Dr. Nis. The man was dedicated to the cause, and he had insisted that he wanted no glory for his contributions when he had joined Kalidonian's inner circle. He preferred anonymity.

Still, the former industrialist was reluctant to spend so large a sum without proof, and now Kalidonian and his key aides were traveling north to the hills that separated Thailand from Burma and Laos to see a demonstration of what they were about to purchase.

He turned to the man who sat in front of him. Marco was German, athletically built, but unlike many of his countrymen, he was quite olive skinned.

"Where is the test taking place, Marco?"

"A small village in the foothills north of here. We should be there in an hour at most," he added.

"And the men you recruited to run the test—can they be trusted?"

Marco nodded, his face revealing his confidence. "Over the years, we have helped one another fight for justice," he answered.

What Marco Gussman didn't add was that they were members of the Vietnamese secret police. He had met them when they had come to what was then East Germany to train with the Stasi, the East German secret police, of which he had been a lieutenant.

His speciality had been assassinations. It was a subject he knew well. He had practiced it for many years, with guns, knives, using piano wire as a garrote and poison.

He had even gone to Moscow to learn how to use such instant-reaction poisons like ricin, which the KGB had used against escaped dissidents.

When the anti-Communists took over the government and started arresting members of the Stasi, the forty-year-old Marco had escaped to Stockholm, where he became involved with fanatic, antigovernment environmental groups.

He had met Kalidonian there after a rally, and offered him his services. He had omitted mentioning his prime qualification—his experience in killing without detection.

But that's the way things went, Marco reminded himself. One had to adjust to the new needs of the changing times. He looked up with an open-eyed, candid look when Kalidonian spoke again.

"How many men did you recruit?"

"Enough to run the test and prevent anyone from interfering with it."

Marco didn't explain that the source of interference he referred to had been identified by Dr. Nis. His name was John Hogan, and he had some connection with United States Intelligence. A former member of the American Special Forces, the man lived in a Cambodian Buddhist temple six hundred miles from the test site.

"Good," Kalidonian said. As he turned to the attractive woman sitting beside him, some extra energy seemed to fill his short, stout body. "Isn't it good, Karla?"

"Yes, it's wonderful," the young brunette replied nervously. She hadn't been told what kind of test was being planned or how it fit into his plans to force the world to give in to his demands for environmental reform.

"What kind of test is this going to be?"

Kalidonian patted her hand. "You'll see."

"I wish you had let me bring my video camera," she complained.

"There will be a lot of things you can tape for your network to broadcast when we go public," he promised in a gentle tone.

Karla Hamilton had also sneaked a tiny palm-sized Minox camera into her purse, but she could see no way to take pictures without arousing the old man's suspicions.

She had been Kalidonian's close companion since he had met her at the press conference at the start of construction of the biosphere community he had named Gaia. A correspondent for the World Cable News network, she had taken a leave of absence from her network and volunteered her services to the retired billionaire.

Kalidonian adjusted his fawn-colored jumpsuit, then patted Marco on the shoulder. "You have done well, my friend."

To the man who was sitting alone in the rear of the helicopter, he said, "You too, Nis. You seem to have everything under control." He turned to Karla again. "Doesn't he, Karla?"

"It seems so," she replied without much enthusiasm.

"Well, tell him so."

Bracing herself, the brunette turned her head and tried to force a smile as she looked at Dr. Nis. There was something about him that made her feel uncomfortable. She wasn't sure what it was, but she knew that her uneasiness was caused by something more than his too-yellow blond hair or his strange Oriental eyes.

Karla also didn't trust the scientist, and she thought she knew why. Unlike other men who had difficulty masking their lust for her, he looked at her as if she were some alien specimen he would like to dissect and examine under a microscope.

Still, she couldn't ignore Kalidonian's request if she wanted him to continue trusting her.

"You seem to have everything under control, Dr. Nis," Karla said, thinking that she sounded like a parrot. A small voice inside of her kept warning that this story might be too big even for her.

Nis acknowledged the compliment with a perfunctory nod. His mind was too busy with other matters, and he didn't bother concerning himself with her obvious dislike for him.

He had originally considered conducting the test on the temple in Angkor Wat where the creature named Hogan spent his time, but the choice would have aroused Kalidonian's suspicions prematurely.

Kalidonian's excited voice interrupted his thoughts. "Look down there at the ground," he shouted, then ordered the pilot to fly just above the trees.

The occupants of the helicopter pressed their faces against the windows and looked down at the thatched-roof huts clustered closely together in a clearing.

Stands of bamboo and thick foliage surrounded the area. A communal fire still burned in a fireplace crudely constructed of rocks and mud.

A small group of pajama-clad men were gathered around a missile launcher high on a hill overlooking the village. As the helicopter flew over, they looked up and waved, then sent a canister spiraling toward the cluster of houses.

The round metal can crashed on the dirt clearing near a communal well.

A woman and child drawing water looked at the canister, then up at the helicopter hovering above.

Suddenly they started tearing at their faces and bodies. Just as suddenly their desperate attempts to tear away invisible demons stopped, and they fell to the ground in a twisted heap.

Everywhere the airborne passengers looked, there were the newly dead bodies of men, women and children. A young boy lay still, his hand still clutching the tiny pink ear of a dead piglet. Near him a wiry-looking man still grasped the stock of his ancient musket, his finger pressing against the rusting trigger that he would never fire again.

A young man and woman, half-hidden behind a stand of rattan, were locked together in an intimate embrace.

Around the corpses were the carcasses of several dozen pigs and chickens. Everything living had been wiped out in a matter of minutes.

Still lying where it fell, the large khaki-colored aerosol canister was identified as the property of the United States government by the large white lettering on it.

Karla tore herself away from the window, grabbed the air sickness bag from the pocket of the seat in front of her and began to throw up.

Kalidonian's face was filled with sadness. "Tragic, but necessary," he muttered. To Marco he said in a choked voice, "Do you think they're all dead?"

"I would think so," came the reply.

The man in the fawn gray jumpsuit took a deep breath. "Tell the suppliers we will pay their fee on delivery, Marco."

Then he summoned a smile as he turned to Dr. Nis. "In thirty days the world will have to accept my terms."

Alexander Nis merely nodded. Everything was on schedule.

4

John Hogan knew he was dreaming, but it was one of his better dreams. This one was not filled with violence and death, with dismembered bodies and distorted carcasses.

His face reflected a rare contentment. The harsh, intimidating mask had softened as he dreamed of Astrah.

They were in a bed someplace in Brom's palace in Kalabria. Astrah was nestled in his arms, her strawberry-colored hair pushed against his face.

"The life of a warrior's woman is lonely and difficult, Hogan," she whispered. There was no complaint in the tone. "But you make up for it when you return."

"I come back as often as I can," he heard himself reply, though not in apology. It was a restatement of fact.

As hard as he tried, he had not yet mastered the ability to transfer himself through time and dimension to her world at will.

He could only travel to where she was when the shimmering cloud materialized. And it only did so when Brom was in danger, as it did for Brom when Hogan faced peril.

Astrah's face began to fade from his dream to be replaced by another one. Brom's.

Hogan fully expected to see the red-bearded brawler in the midst of a battle. That was how he usually pictured Brom, wielding the huge sword, outnumbered by screaming soldiers or fanatic savages intent on slaying him.

But no, the warrior was asleep in his bed, tossing as if he were in the middle of a nightmare.

Hogan was certain that Brom was in some danger. But from whom?

He sat up in his bed and looked around the room that had been his home for so long.

There was no shimmering cloud waiting to transport him to the Kalabrian's side.

This time it really must have been only a dream, he decided, and let his head sink back on the small, cotton-filled pillow. He slept for a long time, until he woke to a soft hammering on the wooden door to his room. Hogan reached down to the ground and pulled his 9 mm Beretta from his holster.

"Yes?"

The door slowly opened, revealing a slight figure in saffron robes standing in the doorway. His forehead was still covered with bandages from the bullet wound, and perched proudly on his nose were his new steel-rimmed glasses.

Mok Seng's face was a mask of sternness. "You sleep your life away," he said crisply.

The American yawned and stretched, trying to ease his aching back muscles. "What's up?"

"You should be. It is time for your lesson." He paused. "Already it is an hour later than it should be."

Black Jack groaned. Even though he had made it clear he had no intention of ever becoming a Buddhist monk, the abbot had decided he would spend some of each day learning the *Dharmasuksa*—the course of Buddhist studies for the lay person—and the ways of the spiritual warrior.

Wary, he asked, "Is this going to be a spiritual or physical lesson?"

"All lessons are spiritual. Some just hurt your unused muscles more than others."

The American pulled himself out of the narrow cot and slid the automatic into its holster.

"Always you must travel with the weapons of death. Have you learned no peace here?"

Ignoring the comment, Hogan gathered up his CAR-15 automatic rifle and his krall, then he donned a pair of black peasant pants and a thin black shirt.

He could feel the muscles of his back screaming with pain.

The tiny hard cot was never intended for someone his height, but all of his protests that he needed a larger bed had fallen on unsympathetic ears.

Slipping into a pair of sandals made from discarded rubber tires, Black Jack checked his face in the sliver of mirror on the wall.

He saw the long lean face that showed his mixed heritage of Apache and Scot, and the startlingly pale blue eyes that both fascinated and frightened anyone who looked into them.

There was a hint of whiskers on his face, and he started to reach for the straight razor.

"Later," Mok Seng ordered. "There are no women waiting to admire you. Especially the one from the other world."

Embarrassed, Hogan regretted telling the monk about Astrah.

Quickly he combed his long dark blond hair with his fingers and turned back to face his mentor.

Clasping his hands together in front of his face, he bowed to the Buddhist monk as a sign of respect, then followed him out of his cell.

"Datza!" Black Jack Hogan shouted as the meaty fist slammed into his stomach.

The assailant, a young saffron-robed monk, bowed and stepped back. A second young monk, fatter than the first, moved forward, then crouched and charged full force with his head at the American's midsection.

"Datza!" Hogan screamed even louder as the next attack pushed him backward a half-dozen steps. He caught himself before his bare feet slipped on the wet grass.

The monsoon rains had just started, and the steady mist of water soaked his thick hair and clothes. The weapons he had set down on one of the elephant's ear leaves that the locals used as raincoats were getting drenched despite the fact he had covered them with several of the giant fronds.

He would have to spend hours drying the CAR-15 automatic rifle, the 9 mm Beretta 92-F pistol and the eighteen-inch krall. Even the musette bag he carried, which contained extra clips for the two guns, was soaked.

All Hogan wanted to do was get out of the rain and back into the room he occupied in the small temple that stood a hundred yards away.

Hogan saw Mok Seng, who had been observing the battle from under a large, lemon yellow umbrella, come toward him. He postponed thoughts of getting dry as he began to tense his stomach muscles.

"No. Relax your stomach," Mok Seng called out, his voice tinged with disapproval. "Already you forget what I have taught you."

Without warning, he twisted his body and delivered a bone-splintering kick to the American's solar plexus.

"Datza!" Hogan yelled with earsplitting volume as the callused heel hammered at his inner organs and shoved him to the ground.

He lay on the ground, panting and letting his body adjust to the new pain. Holding the umbrella above his head, Mok Seng stood over Hogan and scowled.

"What is it you were shouting?"

"Datza."

"What kind of word is that? Your American slang?"

"Apache."

Mok Seng's tone changed from sarcastic to interested. "What does this word mean?"

"Die."

"I should have known. That is all you think about. Killing and dying." He shook his head. "Get up. There will be time to rest later, you lazy *pnong*."

As he turned away and mumbled instructions to the other two, John Hogan slowly pulled himself to his feet. Despite the pain he felt, he looked down at the slight monk and forced a cynical smile on his face. "What is it I was supposed to have learned, little grandfather?"

"If you shout just before the attacker makes contact with your stomach, the muscles between your stomach and your chest are already pulled in. Then if you hold your breath in, you strengthen your stomach muscles and dissipate much of the force of the blow. You must use your lungs and voice when you fight."

Black Jack Hogan listened carefully. Everything he could learn that would help him survive in a profession where death was a daily companion was valuable. As a special agent who reported directly to the President's Intelligence aide, Hogan was assigned any mission that couldn't be handled through normal channels.

"Now the second lesson," Mok Seng said. "I want you to study the three of us."

"Why are you pushing so hard on my lessons today, little grandfather?"

For once Mok Seng didn't frown at the American's nickname. Instead, his usually emotionless expression softened, and he looked sad.

"Soon you will need every skill you can learn."

There was an ominous tone in his voice.

"What have you heard?"

The small man shook his head. "Not heard. Sensed." He suddenly looked frail. "There is a wind coming that will destroy us all." He shrugged. "Perhaps not even you can stop it."

He started to walk away, then stopped and turned back. His eyes suddenly shone with an angry fire. "But you must try, *pnong*. So it is written in your destiny."

Then he gestured to the other two monks.

Puzzled, Hogan stared at the three Cambodians. The younger two were barely out of their teens. Probably they were fulfilling their family responsibility by joining a Buddhist order for several months. They looked uncomfortable as Black Jack studied them.

Mok Seng looked at Hogan.

"What do you see?"

Hogan shrugged. "I see three monks in saffron robes."

"What else do you see?"

The American glanced around. "The temple. The jungle." He turned his head. "The road that runs along the outside of the ruins. The—"

The abbot snapped an irritated interruption. "What else do you see when you look at us?"

"Three men who just pounded the hell out of my stomach."

"You are not trying, Hogan." The monk was angry.

Black Jack sighed. "What else am I supposed to see?"

"You *should* see that each of us has two parts. The animal in us, which other animals can see. And the spiritual, which a warrior must learn to see." He took a deep breath. "Try," he ordered.

The American focused on the two younger monks, but all he saw was two wet young men who showed their discomfort about being studied. Then he took in Mok Seng.

He could see the animal in the venerable monk. Despite Mok Seng's frail facade, Hogan had seen him easily overcome three younger opponents in a contest.

"Open your mind, *pnong*. Because you lack understanding, it does not mean something does not exist."

Hogan took a deep breath and closed his eyes to relax them. Then he opened them and studied the abbot again.

There was something else about Mok Seng. A glowing aura easily twice his size that loomed about him. It was as if the tiny Cambodian were surrounded by the wisdom of the ages.

Black Jack's expression softened. "I think I understand. What now?"

"Turn your back to us."

The American did so.

"You should be able to see all three of us."

Hogan tried to see the three monks in his mind.

"Okay," he said. "I think I've got a fix on you."

"We will try to pull you to the ground. You must try to evade us." There was a pause, then he added, "Without turning around."

Hogan nodded. Maybe after this next lesson, he could pick up his weapons and get them and himself dry.

He listened for the soft sounds of bare feet moving toward him from behind. But all he heard was the steady subtle hammering of the rain on the foliage.

The leanly built young monk dived at the American's feet in an attempt to pull him to the ground. Hogan hopped to one side, leaving the Cambodian to clutch at a handful of wet grass.

The second monk leapt high into the air, trying to land a kick at the side of Hogan's head. Moments before his bare feet and the American's head came into contact, Black Jack spun out of the way, and the monk tumbled to the ground.

Feeling more confident, Hogan started to turn around, then felt a stunning blow against the side of his head. His legs went dead beneath him, and he collapsed like an empty paper bag.

Blood rushed through his eyes, blurring his vision. Finally the throbbing in his head subsided, and he looked up.

Mok Seng was standing above him, smiling. "You have learned your lesson well, Hogan."

With the monk's help, Hogan got to his feet. "But you were able to take me by surprise."

Mok Seng patted his back. "I said you learned your lesson well. You have not mastered it yet."

Hogan reached down and retrieved his weapons.

"Now can I get dry?"

"After you have sat and meditated on your lesson."

Black Jack was about to protest, then studied the firm expression on the monk's face.

Surrendering, he tore an elephant's ear leaf from a nearby vine and wrapped it around his shoulders. Squatting down on the soupy ground, he crossed his legs into the lotus position and looked up.

"Where will you be?"

Mok Seng adjusted his yellow umbrella and started to walk back to the temple.

"Inside, getting dry," he called out over his shoulder. "I am not the one who has learned a lesson."

For a moment the American decided to defy the abbot and retreat to his warm, cell-like room. He gathered his weapons and started to rise when he saw Mok Seng pause at the heavy wooden door to the temple and gaze at him.

Hogan froze in his half-risen position and glared back. Calm, expressionless eyes met his gaze unblinkingly.

Black Jack surrendered and sat back down on the wet grass. He shut his eyes and tried to meditate, but all that he could manage to visualize were memories.

A kaleidoscope of memories.

His lonely upbringing on an Arizona ranch as the son of a Scots rancher and Apache mother.

The missions during the war when he led a squad of counterinsurgency specialists on Intelligence raids throughout Southeast Asia.

His medical discharge near the end of the war, and the discovery that he was considered too unstable to be trusted with the knowledge he had of secret Intelligence operations. The decision by his own superiors to eliminate him as a solution.

The intervention by his former Indochinese contact, Hiram Wilson, now the White House's Intelligence aide, who recruited him as his personal field agent.

The Khmer Rouge attack two years earlier that left him dead—or nearly dead.

And the strange dreams of Brom and Kalabria, which turned out not to be dreams at all but the beginning of a new existence without the boundaries of time or dimension.

Quite some time had elapsed when Hogan decided he was ready to leave his thoughts and return to the warmth of the temple interior.

He got to his feet and suddenly sensed he was no longer alone. He stared into the jungle around him, but the steaming rains had created a wall of mist that made it almost impossible to see past the trees.

Still he knew there was something out there.

An animal—or was it another enemy?

He had faced many since he had accepted the position Wilson had offered him. Power-crazy warlords and dictators, terrorists and traitors, and some even he could not define.

Like the creature who called himself Nis.

Brom and he had fought together to destroy him. But even after he had been thwarted in his attempts to conquer both their worlds, the creature merely vanished.

He grabbed his weapons. Belting his Model 92-F Beretta around his waist, he slipped the krall into the scabbard that hung from the holster belt, then prepared his CAR-15 automatic.

His mind and body suddenly on full alert, he listened for the faintest sound.

Then he heard it. The soft rustle of a single leaf.

Hogan spun around, his right index finger already pulling back on the trigger of the CAR-15 in his hands.

That's when he saw the transparent shimmering cloud, floating slightly off the ground.

5

Hogan smiled and relaxed his finger as he looked at the radiant fog. This was no enemy. This was . . .

He stopped. Where was Brom? The center of the cloud was empty.

"Behind you," a deep voice called.

Hogan turned and saw Brom, looking as solid as the earth and holding the mammoth howling sword that was as much a part of him as his arms and legs.

Slung across his shoulder he wore the AK-47 he had brought back from Hogan's world.

"You have become careless, Hogan," he admonished.

"How so?"

Brom gestured for the American to follow him through a mist-filled stand of foliage. Two sword-shattered bodies lay among the bushes. One was headless.

"Do you recognize them?"

"No. Probably bandits. There have been reports of raids on villages in the area."

Black Jack studied the face of the one who still had his head. Then realized his features weren't Cambodian. He looked like the squad that attacked him outside of Battambang.

Vietnamese.

"Why would they attack a religious place?"

Hogan was just about to explain that he was just as puzzled when he saw movement from a corner of his eye.

The "corpse" who had retained his head was cradling his AK-47 automatic rifle in his hands and pointing it at the back of the red-bearded warrior.

With a scream of rage and pain, the gunman forced his finger against the trigger of his weapon.

Hogan turned his CAR-15 quickly and half emptied his clip of death-seekers past the giant swordsman. The lead slugs exploded inside the chest of the fallen man and released a shower of spurting red fluid.

Surprised, the Kalabrian spun around and saw the shattered body behind him. With a swift movement he held his huge blade in front of him as he carefully surveyed the forest.

An elephant's ear was shivering, and howling with rage, Brom charged at it.

Hogan saw the tip of an automatic rifle through the thick foliage. Swinging his CAR-15 around, he sprayed the vine of Elephant's Ear with the rest of the slugs in his clip.

A scream from behind the foliage was cut short as two of the tumblers tore into the face and neck of the hidden assailant.

Ignoring the human carcass that fell at his feet, Brom shouted "Die!" as he cut through the thick ropes of vines and growth in front of him with the howling sword.

Cowering against the thick trunk of a vine-covered tree, another assassin in black peasant clothes tried to turn the AK-47 in his hands at the charging giant.

Brom grasped his giant weapon with both hands and slashed at the terrified man. The razor-sharp blade nearly severed the small man in two as blood formed a pool of crimson gore around his feet.

Staring in shock, the man tried to staunch the flow of blood, then suddenly gave up the impossible task and fell forward.

Black Jack dropped his gun and knelt before the dying attacker.

"Why were you trying to kill me?"

The man kept wheezing as he tried to force out the words.

"Nothing can stop us now. You and your kind are dead," he mumbled, then gurgled and choked on the blood filling his throat.

The American shook the man's shoulders. "What do you mean? Talk!"

A hollow sound rumbled from inside the fallen man's throat. Then his head slumped, and his eyes stared sightlessly up at sky.

Brom returned and waited nearby for Black Jack to stand. "What did he tell you?"

Hogan sounded puzzled. "Nothing that makes sense."

"Very little in your world does," the Kalabrian commented, then picked up the automatic rifle the American had dropped and handed it over.

"Two of the poison pellets would have been sufficient to stop him," he admonished.

Despite the anger he felt over the surprise attack, Hogan laughed. "This from somebody who runs out of ammunition regularly?"

"If you were to bring an adequate supply when you came, there would not be a problem of having enough poison pellets in my fire-stick."

The American stopped the discussion. No matter how often he had lectured the other warrior, the concept that guns needed bullets in order to work seemed beyond him.

While Brom cleaned his blade with a piece of cloth torn from the attire of one of the dead men, Hogan carefully checked the area to see if he could find out who had sent them.

He found a surplus half-ton truck of Vietnam vintage parked at the side of the narrow highway. He searched the interior but the only thing it yielded was another map, similar to the one he had found before.

Black Jack rejoined Brom, who examined him carefully. "You are not wounded?"

Hogan shook his head. "Thanks for coming to my assistance," he said gratefully.

"That was not why I came," the Kalabrian admitted.

Black Jack's face showed his surprise.

"Are you having problems of your own in Kalabria again?"

"Yes. Many of the hired soldiers who lived after following the alien creature have returned under the horned banner of a would-be conqueror named Peytok, who is trying to capture control of Kalabria."

"And you need my help."

"No."

The American was startled at the reply. Why else was his red-bearded spiritual twin here?

"Zhuzak and the army can deal with them."

Black Jack had wrestled with Zhuzak for sport at a feast, and although he had won the match against the powerfully built warrior, Hogan's ribs ached every time he remembered the bout.

"I'll put my money on him," he agreed. "Then you came to help me. Thanks."

Brom glanced at the dead assassins. "You are welcome, but you could have dealt with them without my aid. No, that was not the main reason I came."

The Kalabrian's words confused Black Jack.

"I have come to ask you to return with me for a meeting with Mondlock," he explained.

"Any special reason? Is Astrah with . . . with child?"

"No, no. She misses you, but she is as vigorous as ever. Mondlock will not explain what until you are with me. Only that something terrible is about to happen."

"Is the threat from this character Peytok?"

"No. Something else. Whatever it is, it has Mondlock frightened."

Black Jack could not imagine anything terrifying the wise man.

He wanted to ask Brom another question, then saw that Brom had stepped into the center of the shimmering cloud. Quickly Hogan gathered his weapons and joined him.

As he moved into the center of the glowing, Black Jack thought of the Buddhist abbot's warning.

There is a wind coming that will destroy us all, Mok Seng had said. *Perhaps not even you can save us. But you must try.*

As the shimmering cloud closed in around them, Hogan began to shiver. He knew it was not from his still-damp clothing.

6

Captain Nicholas Matusis knew he was caught between a rock and a hard place as he stared up at the darkening clouds through the storm-splattered windows of the bridge. The Naval Weather Service had been issuing storm warnings to ships in the Central Pacific for the past twelve hours.

He contacted Johnston Atoll for orders.

"We're under a tight timetable," the officer in charge said crisply. "The environmentalists would like nothing better than to stop us, so I'd prefer you stayed on course. But I can't ask you to risk the crew if this turns into a typhoon. You'll have to decide if you can ride out the storm or if you should change course and try to escape."

The cargo ship skipper understood. There had been a tremendous amount of controversy about this voyage in both the American and foreign press. The fanatic fringes of the environmental movements had threatened to use whatever force they needed to stop the movement of the dead cargo.

He appreciated the military's concerns about their schedule. But he had the safety of his crew and his ship to consider.

"I'll monitor weather conditions, then make a decision," Matusis advised, then signed off.

He stared at the boiling sea outside the portholes and rubbed the dark stubble of beard on his chin. As he weighed his decision, he could feel the massive waves hitting the ship along the side and making it roll. He was positive it would get worse. Much worse.

This was typhoon season. Nick Matusis had never been caught in one of the giant ocean storms despite his thirty years at sea. The cargo ship skipper had credited his good fortune to his Greek mother, who claimed she was a direct descendant of the Greek goddess of luck, Tyche.

Now he wasn't so sure his luck hadn't run out. His ship, the *Murman,* was a Norwalk class cargo ship operated by the Military Sealift Command. Although she could carry as many as sixteen vertically stowed Poseidon missiles, she wasn't heavy enough to withstand the torment of an assault by a typhoon.

Even if he thought that the *Murman* could withstand the storm, there was too much risk that the cargo wouldn't. If it didn't, then it was all over for him, for his crew and probably for every person within five hundred miles of the ship.

He thought his first officer, Fahey McCarter, would agree, although the first officer had been more withdrawn than usual ever since most of the large military convoy that had escorted them from Europe and through the Panama Canal had departed when they passed the Hawaiian Islands.

"Probably worrying about the cargo we're carrying," Nick reminded himself. Like his first officer, Matusis had been in daily dread of an accident that would activate the more than six thousand tons of death stored in the hold below.

The ship's cargo consisted of one hundred thousand shells filled with VX and GB, many of which were already mixed and ready to be launched. In addition, there were several thousand pressurized cannisters of the poison gas components—enough to wipe out the Earth's population three times.

The material had been stored by the American military in a top secret depot in the southwestern German city of

Clauen as part of the United States' mutual defense agreement with NATO. When the United States and Soviet Union signed an arms reduction pact, it entailed a decision to reduce the number of chemical weapons.

While the carefully screened contract crew had sailed their empty cargo ship across the North Atlantic to the North Sea port of Nordenam to pick up the deadly cargo, rumors started that environmental fanatics were scheming to steal the deadly missiles.

A massive protection force, including fifteen hundred police officers, a small army of sharpshooters and a team of helicopter spotters, had been assembled and escorted the convoy to the port.

Once the cargo had been loaded on the *Murman,* two squads of armed chemical warfare specialists, under the command of Colonel Arthur Lesser, joined the crew for the long sea voyage.

As a contract captain to the Military Sealift Command, Matusis was committed to delivering the shells to the atoll, which was located 825 miles southwest of Honolulu.

There was a substantial bonus for him and his crew if the cargo was delivered on schedule.

After being unloaded at Johnston Island, the shells and their contents would be destroyed by experts in a newly built chemical weapons incinerator.

Captain Matusis studied the latest weather reports, grabbing hold of the edge of the table to steady himself against the roiling water. Then he glanced up at the large clock.

It was time for his first officer and him to inspect the cargo again as part of the four daily checks he had instituted.

He sent a member of the crew to fetch the other man from his quarters.

FAHEY MCCARTER SAT on the edge of his bunk and stared at the four men crowded into his tiny quarters. The thick, black eyebrows that framed his piercing dark eyes quivered as he fondled a round plastic object the size of a regulation baseball.

All were trained professionals. Former Navy commandos, they now hired out their services to whoever could afford the fee. McCarter had worked with each of them on past missions.

Tim Ludmann, his thin face intent while he stared at the plastic object, lifted his eyes to McCarter's.

"How do we handle this one?"

"Like the opium hijacking last year."

The five of them had worked together on that mission. Thirty-seven tons of refined opium had been transported by trucks from the hills of the Golden Triangle where Burma, Laos and Thailand touched to the tiny Burmese port of Pyapon. There a freighter was to carry the multibillion-dollar cargo to a small port in Baja, California. McCarter had signed on as first mate, the other four as crew members.

As the freighter had sailed out of the Andaman Sea and into the Indian Ocean, they had shot and killed the captain and the rest of the crew, then delivered the cargo to one of the small islands just outside of Hong Kong, where leaders of the Chinese syndicate who had hired them were waiting to take over.

McCarter hadn't known where the Chinese planned to sell the opium. Nor did he know what Marco Gussman and his associates planned to do with the shells and canisters. And he didn't care.

He and his team had been hired to do a job, and they were about to earn their money.

"We had guns on the opium job," Jack Hadley, a bald, barrel-chested man, reminded McCarter.

"Yeah," seconded Peter Dressler. He had an open, friendly-looking face, but his eyes had a constant, hooded quality.

"We've got something better," the first mate replied, holding up the plastic ball in his hand.

Casually he tossed it to Ludmann. Fumbling for a moment, he managed to catch the object.

"Good thing you caught that," McCarter said with a sardonic smile. "There's enough poison gas inside it to wipe out a small town."

The man who had caught the ball almost dropped it at McCarter's words. Quickly he handed it back to the first officer.

"Tonight we plant these in all the crew quarters, along with a timer to set off the small explosive trigger hidden inside each one," the first officer added.

Jake Braun shifted his compact frame uncomfortably in the chair. "I didn't sign on to get killed. How do we protect ourselves? Contamination suits?"

McCarter shook his head. "They'd arouse suspicions. No. We detonate the balls from the bridge deck after everybody's gone below."

Ludmann looked unhappy. "What about those who are on watch?"

The first mate set the ball down on his bunk and reached under his pillow. In his hand was a ballpoint pen.

"You kill them with one of these."

The four men stared at the penlike object in the first officer's right hand.

"What is it?"

"A dart gun. The tips of the dart are covered with ricin."

Marco Gussman had provided a quantity of the deadly writing instruments.

They all knew about the powerful poison that could kill a large man in fifteen minutes. It was part of the knowledge that came with experience in their chosen profession.

"I prefer an Uzi to a damn ballpoint pen," the barrel-chested man growled.

"And have those two destroyers escorting us send a boarding party over to find out who fired the shots?"

Dressler shook his head. "What about the storm?"

"It shouldn't be in full force until late tomorrow. By then we'll be already sailing south," McCarter replied as he brought out a cardboard box filled with the pens.

He distributed the pens, then opened the top of a large aluminum case. The others glanced down.

Inside were eight plastic balls and timers.

He handed a pair to each of the men.

"Make sure that all crew quarters—including that of the military contingent—are covered."

"What about us?" The question came from Ludmann.

He nodded. "Set the timers for two hours from now." There was a knock on his cabin door, and he rose to his feet.

"We'll seal the doors in two hours. So make sure you're on the bridge before then."

He opened the door to his cabin. One of the crew was waiting for him.

"The captain sent for you, sir."

OUTSIDE, the wind was brisk. Violent gusts attacked the water, turning the sea choppy. A thin veil of rain was driven by the storm to slash against the *Murman*.

On the bridge Captain Matusis was waiting for the first officer.

McCarter, wearing dripping rain gear, entered the cabin.

"Smells like it could turn into a typhoon to me, Captain. I think we'd better get our tails out of here."

"No. We'll ride it out," Matusis replied after weighing McCarter's words. He turned to the helmsman. "Hold her steady on course."

McCarter glowered for a moment, then erased the expression of irritation from his face.

"You sent for me. What's up?"

"I want you to accompany me on an inspection of the cargo. I just want to make sure everything's tied down."

COLONEL ARTHUR LESSER and his team sat on the edge of their bunks, looking green. All twelve of them had been on the verge of becoming seasick ever since the storm had begun to rock the cargo ship. As a specialist in chemical and biological weapons—or CBWs—Colonel Lesser had spent most of his Army career around all kinds of CBWs. But never before on a ship. And, until this voyage, never around already mixed chemical weapons—except in controlled test environments.

Typically the components in chemical and biological weapons were kept separate until just before launching. The career officer didn't know what had prompted the authorities to mix them in the batch of shells stored below, but it made his assignment more dangerous.

Not that he was afraid of risks. His entire military career had been spent in the presence of experimental weapons. From the time the Special Operations Group had plucked him from his tenured teaching-and-research position at the Massachusetts Institute of Technology, Lesser had helped develop and test a variety of chemical and biological weapons to neutralize the impact of similar developments in the Soviet Union and among some of the more fanatic Middle Eastern dictatorships.

Since the government's decision to reduce their stockpile of CBWs, Lesser had announced his decision to return to teaching.

This was his last mission as a senior member of the top secret Special Operations Group.

Heading up a hand-picked force of experienced Special Forces professionals, Lesser's assignment was to prevent any attempts to derail the deadly cargo from its final destination. In the hands of terrorists or zealous environmentalist groups—both of whom had publicly threatened to try to steal the shells and hold the world hostage—the poison gas missiles could eliminate every living creature in the world.

During the voyage they had worked in four-man teams, maintaining an armed twenty-four-hour vigil.

Their journey had taken them across the North Atlantic, then down through the Panama Canal and into the Pacific Ocean. Accompanied by a flotilla of escort vessels filled with training military personnel, their voyage had been uneventful.

As they passed the outer Hawaiian Islands, most of the vessels left them to head for Pearl Harbor. For the last eight hundred miles of the voyage, they were being escorted by a pair of light destroyers.

And by the storm outside.

Lesser swallowed the bile he could feel coming up from his stomach and looked at his men.

"Whose shift is it?"

Weakly, Lieutenant Younger raised his hand. "Mine, sir."

The colonel tried to force a smile on his wan face. "You look like shit, Lieutenant."

"Begging your pardon, Colonel, but so do you."

There were weak laughs from several of the other men in their quarters.

Lesser forced himself to his feet. "I'll take the shift, Younger."

The lieutenant looked up at the senior officer. "If you think I'm going to argue with you, sir, you're nuts."

As he looked around to pick the three men who'd join him in his watch, Lesser noticed the wired plastic ball sitting on a shelf.

"What's that?"

Younger glanced at the plastic ball.

"One of the crew brought it in while you were at dinner, sir. Something to do with getting ready to fumigate the ship after we land."

"Well, nobody play with it. Who knows what kind of insecticide they've got in it," the colonel ordered.

As if it was reacting to his words, the ball suddenly exploded, and the soft sound of escaping gas filled the bunk room.

"What the hell—" Lieutenant Younger's words stuck in his throat as he tore at his face and neck, then suddenly slid to the floor.

He was dead. Like the other eleven men in the room.

As the storm continued to batter the freighter, Captain Matusis led the way along the deck to the gangway that led to the holds where the shells had been stored. He kept a tight grip on the handrails to keep his balance on the heaving vessel. Behind him First Officer McCarter did the same.

"Might be smart to change your mind and get out of this damn storm," McCarter shouted over the wind.

"We've got a schedule to maintain," Matusis insisted stubbornly.

"The schedule's been changing," Fahey McCarter said coldly as he leaned forward and rammed the modified ballpoint pen in his hand into the captain's neck.

He watched as the body slid to the deck, then turned and saw his men clutching the rails against the wildly rolling sea.

Working his way back to them along the rails, he gathered them into a tight circle.

"Time to get rid of the rest of the crew and head south."

Ludmann turned his head and stared at the naval vessels tossing about in the brewing storm.

"What about the Navy ships?"

McCarter looked up at the sky.

"We'll wait until dark. They'll be too busy trying to survive the storm to realize we're gone until it's too late."

He checked his wristwatch, then faced them again.

"I've got a call to make."

7

Black Jack Hogan was in Brom's world. He looked around at the familiar landscape. It was different from his own world, yet in many ways similar.

The vegetation's color wasn't the same, and neither was the water that flowed in the rivers of Kalabria.

Hogan stared fondly at the neon green grassy plains and gentle rolling hills of Kalabria, surrounded by high mountains to the east, west and north.

He studied the plains, broken by patches of wooded areas that stretched for countless miles to the range of cobalt blue mountains in the distance. He could barely make out the dense forests that separated the tall grass country from the towering peaks.

Overhead, twin moons began to make their appearance in the lavender-tinted sky.

The inhabitants were at a different stage of development than those of Earth but who was to say they were really any worse off? The people he had met on past journeys here, both the good and the bad, were driven by the same basic human desires he had known in his own world. They had their dreams, their hopes, their fears and their needs. Children still played at make-believe games, and their mothers still worried about them. Women became wives and men husbands. And among them were those, much the way it was on Earth, who would sacrifice everything for power and wealth.

Then there was Brom.

Hogan had fought at his side against those who had tried to destroy the land the warrior's ancestors had ruled for almost a thousand years. And joined him in joyous celebrations after they were victorious. They had shared happiness and tragedy and found their bond growing stronger with each experience. In Brom, the American found the only true friend he had known.

Hogan glanced at the warrior who rode at his side. Brom was strangely silent. Before anyone could discover their departure, the pair had slipped out of the capital city of Tella through a small, rarely used gate and were following the high road north of the walled city.

Hogan wondered where they were going. Finally he asked.

"A small hamlet four hours from here," Brom replied, "to meet Mondlock."

The American had been surprised to learn that the Knower had left the city without warning before Hogan had arrived. But waiting for them was the young white-haired boy they had once saved from death by marauding mercenaries.

Hogan thought it was strange for Mondlock to pick so distant a place for a meeting.

"What's there?"

Brom shook his head. "I don't know. But Mondlock left a note with Timur for us to meet him there."

Hogan looked back at the solemn-faced boy who sat proudly in a scaled-down saddle mounted on the back of a fierce-looking animal. In his waistband the eleven-year-old wore a smaller version of the long knife Kalabrian warriors carried as a symbol of their manhood. The weapon had been given to him by Hogan and Brom for the courage he had displayed in standing up to the mercenaries.

Hogan wasn't sure what to expect in the small village. But he was ready.

A CAR-15 automatic rifle was strapped to his saddle, and around his waist hung a quick-draw holster with his Beretta and the krall. Hanging from the horn of his saddle was his musette bag with extra clips.

Brom was also armed. He wore his feared double-edged sword in a shoulder harness. His own krall hung from a belt at his waist. Slung across his saddle was one of the AK-47s he had brought back with him from Hogan's world, and a small leather bag with extra clips.

Hogan glanced at Brom. "Why all the secrecy about my being here?"

The Kalabrian had rushed him to the stables where Timur and two saddled horses were waiting when he arrived.

"Mondlock insisted that no one know you were here."

Black Jack had planned to see the woman whose hair was the color of wild strawberries and who had claimed him as her mate.

"I had hoped to spend time with Astrah."

"It will have to wait. Not even Mora knows I have left the city," Brom replied coldly.

Hogan realized that Brom must be very concerned, because usually he kept no secrets from the tall, handsome woman whom he planned to marry some day.

"The sooner we find out what Mondlock is worried about, the sooner we can get it fixed," Hogan remarked. "Then we can get back to Tella, and Astrah and I—"

"From the message he left, I'm not sure it can be—as you put it—fixed," Brom interrupted.

Black Jack had never heard Brom sound so distant.

"We've faced some impossible challenges before," he said, trying to sound reassuring.

"This has something to do with the death of Ost."

Hogan knew that, according to the Kalabrians, Ost was the god who created everything, including the other gods.

Supposedly he lived in the hearts of rare glowing rocks only found in a desolate area of Kalabria called the Forbidden Region. Hogan felt that the rocks contained some radioactive minerals.

No one dared go near the desertlike area at the northern foot of the mountains of the gods. The few who had tried to do so never returned, or, if they did, died horrible screaming deaths shortly afterward.

Kalabrian legends said that poisonous dragons who took the form of rocks inhabited the area and waited to kill unsuspecting travelers.

As one of the handful of wise men who had been selected to be priests of Ost, Mondlock knew where the secret sacred temple to the god was located—and how to pass safely through the desert to reach it.

"Something serious must have come up for Mondlock to rush off and leave us a note," Hogan decided aloud.

Hogan had also read the message the Knower had left behind: "Timur knows how to find me, and you must come to meet me here. It may be too late. Perhaps even the two of you may not be able to save our world from the killing air that is coming."

Again Black Jack remembered Mok Seng's words about the wind that would come to destroy them all. He could feel the hairs on his neck rising.

What did Mok Seng and Mondlock mean? He told Brom what the Buddhist abbot had said.

The huge Kalabrian shook his head. "I don't understand it, either."

The two warriors gestured for Timur to join them.

"Did Mondlock tell you anything about this village?"

"No. A farmer came to see him. Then he wrote this note and left with him." Timur looked worried.

"Is Mondlock in trouble?"

The white-haired boy clenched the small krall at his side. "I don't know. But we should hurry."

Hogan turned to the bearded warrior.

"Did Mondlock tell you anything more before he sent you to get me?"

The Kalabrian shook his head. "No."

"Think. He may have said something you've overlooked."

Suddenly Brom was furious. "I have already told you no!"

Hogan could sense the tension between them. "Then what's bothering you? You're acting as if you're afraid of something. What?"

The Kalabrian grabbed the ornate hilt of his krall. "Are you accusing me of cowardice?"

Hogan reined in his horse and dismounted. His legs spread, he glared up at the warrior towering above him.

"What are you doing?" Brom demanded.

"I'm not traveling another foot," Hogan said, digging the heels of his boots into the hard dirt road, "until you tell me what's bothering you."

"Then I'll go on without you," Brom growled, and turned to the young boy behind them.

"Follow me," he ordered.

"No," Hogan snapped.

Brom seemed to pierce him with his eyes, but Hogan returned his gaze unblinkingly.

"If there is danger, the boy should return to Tella," Hogan continued.

Timur began to protest, but Brom stopped him.

"Hogan is right. You will ride back," he ordered. "Find Commander Zhuzak and tell him to bring a troop of soldiers to the hamlet if he does not hear from me in two sunrises."

Timur started to say something, then studied the hard expressions of the two warriors. Reluctantly he turned his horse around and rode away.

Black Jack waited until they were alone, then faced Brom, his features set.

"I'm waiting for an explanation," he said firmly.

Brom's angry reply was interrupted by the sudden appearance of armed horsemen thundering toward them.

"Death to the Kalabrians!" The black-bearded man leading the charge shouted the war cry as he waved a huge battle-ax and raced his steed at Brom.

Galloping at full speed behind him were eight men wearing horned helmets and fur tunics that made them look like apparitions of the devil as they spurred their horses toward the two defenders.

Brom snatched his krall from its scabbard, then ducked as the heavy metal weapon cleaved the air above him.

Grinning to hide his fury, Brom jammed the eighteen inches of steel through the attacker's thick fur garment and into his solar plexus, then tore upward, severing tissue and blood vessels.

A shower of blood sprayed both men, but the attacker still had some fight left in him. He raised his ax to slash at Brom again, then stared in disbelief as he saw the weapon fall from his unresponsive fingers.

Speechless, he slid from his saddle and landed with a thud on the grass. His horned helmet fell from his lifeless head and tangled the legs of his terrified mount.

Hogan sprang to his horse and tore the CAR-15 free of the straps that held it to the saddle. Jacking a round into the chamber, he braced the automatic weapon against his shoulder and aimed at the two closest assailants, who were brandishing their swords and maces as they raced at him.

Forcing himself to stay calm, he let loose a short burst at the first attacker.

A surprised expression showed on the man's face as a trio of tumblers tore through his neck and head, re-arranging his features into a crimson mass. He tumbled from the saddle and beneath the pounding hoofs of the second assailant.

"Ayee . . . demons!" the second soldier screamed in terror as he tried to turn his overexcited animal away from the man with the fire-spitting weapon.

Hogan had already squeezed off another trio of death-dealers. Hot, soft-nosed slugs severed the attacker's arm and tore into his shoulder. The weapon described a brief arc in the air, and the once-formidable warrior yelled in rage and fear.

"My arm has left me. Help me!"

A second burst of lead ended his suffering, and he was silenced forever.

Brom threw himself at another attacker and, dragging him out of the saddle, threw him on the ground. Falling on top of the assailant, the Kalabrian warrior reached up and slit his throat with a single stroke of his krall.

Pushing the body from him, Brom scrambled to his feet and tore the howling sword from its shoulder scabbard.

He stood next to the fallen body and scanned the area around him. The remaining attackers hesitated for a moment.

"Who wants to die next?" His eyes glowed with excitement as Brom threw out the challenge.

Hogan moved to his side, his CAR-15 covering the enemy.

"Let's get them right now," he muttered, "and not talk them to death."

A couple of the horsemen attempted to move on the two defenders from behind, but Hogan sensed the movement and spun around.

He brought his weapon into play, riddling the men with bullets, and both men slumped over their mounts as the animals took off in a frightened gallop.

The two would-be killers fell from their saddles.

The remaining three stopped their horses and stared in shock. "These are not men but creatures from the dark place," one of them shouted, then turned his horse and spurred him on.

The last two hesitated until Hogan raised his death-spitting weapon. Panic filled their eyes. Sinking their spurs into their mounts, they wheeled them around and fled as if the devil were chasing after them.

Hogan wiped his forehead with his sleeve. He was tempted to sit on the ground and catch his breath, but he knew that rest would have to wait.

"Let's make sure these creeps are dead," he told the Kalabrian.

"Creeps?"

Hogan wasn't up to explaining the word, so he just shrugged and said, "Let's just make sure we won't have a sneak attack."

AS THEY RESTED near their camp fire, Hogan watched Brom study the horned helmet in his hands.

"Anything special about that hat?"

"It is worn by the Nordian soldiers."

"Peytok's country?"

"Yes." Brom stared at the glowing embers. "Nordia is a poor country with not much fertile land. For centuries the people of Nordia have resorted to slipping across borders and stealing from their neighbors. But it was always on a small scale, never enough to arouse the anger of the rulers of the adjacent lands so they would strike back hard at Nordia." Brom paused and threw more logs on the fire.

"That was true until Peytok was crowned," he went on. "There was never enough of anything to make Peytok happy. It didn't matter if it was women, weapons, soldiers, gold or land. Finally even his own people refused to join him in raiding their neighbors merely to fulfill his excessive needs. So Peytok hired warriors from another land to help him. They've tried three times to steal our women and our land, but each time we've watered our crops with their blood. And those who still lived fled back across the borders."

"Is that slimy character back in Kalabria with his gunmen?"

"Slimy?" Brom looked puzzled, then waved a hand. "Never mind. I think I understand what you are trying to say." He took a deep breath. "Apparently Peytok has returned to Kalabria with his forces for another attempt."

"Maybe that's what Mondlock wants to talk about."

"Peytok is a deadly snake. But only a snake." He shook his head. "No, it has to be something much more worrisome."

"Yeah. But what?"

The American warrior had asked the question, but he wasn't sure he wanted to know the answer.

8

"Gone?" Hiram Wilson was stunned. "How can a freighter carrying a hundred thousand shells and canisters disappear?"

The thick Cuban cigar he held in his hand was momentarily forgotten. A long white ash fell on his impeccably tailored jacket unnoticed as the usually soft-spoken official stared aghast at the others in the White House basement conference room.

General Philip Matterling squirmed in his upholstered chair, his eyes glued to the report sitting in front of him on the long walnut conference table. His well-tailored uniform suddenly felt as though it were too tight.

"There was a typhoon in the Central Pacific," the head of the Special Operations Group said apologetically.

Hiram Wilson was skeptical about a storm being responsible for the missing freighter. But then, that was his job. As the White House's Intelligence aide, he was responsible to the President for protecting the United States and its allies from potential enemies.

The deadly cargo of poison gas would give any terrorist or would-be dictator more than enough power to make incredible demands. Or—even worse, if they were so inclined—to unleash enough destruction to virtually eliminate civilization, especially in major cities, where there were concentrations of population.

"Where were the Navy ships escorting the freighter?"

One of the others at the table, Rear Admiral Lewis Demming, shrugged. "They were busy trying to keep from going down in the storm."

"Too busy to keep an eye on the *Murman?*"

"It was dark," the uniformed Naval officer muttered awkwardly.

Wilson turned back to General Matterling.

"How much danger is there that the shells will crack under the pressure of the water—if the freighter did go down?"

"The shells are double walled. They should be able to withstand the pressure."

Next Wilson swirled in his chair and looked inquiringly at the Naval officer who sat to his right.

"How deep is the Pacific at that point?"

"Several miles. But there are a number of underwater mountains in that vicinity. If the cargo vessel got grounded on one of them, it would only be several hundred feet below the surface."

"Assuming—" Wilson put strong emphasis on the word "—the ship did sink, and the shells cracked open, what is the danger, Dr. Weinfield?"

He turned and focused his attention on the fourth man in the room—a tall, balding man in an ill-fitting suit.

Weinfield was in charge of research and development for the Special Operations Group, the top secret military unit responsible for the development and stockpiling of chemical and bacteriological weapons.

"If the majority of shells and canisters did crack open, what would happen?"

"No one knows for sure," Weinfield replied as he studied a series of reports in front of him. "Our best guess is that the waters for a hundred miles around the vessel would be poisoned, probably destroying all sea life in the area."

Wilson wasn't satisfied with the answer. "How long would the danger last?"

"The VX and GB chemicals—"

The Southerner interrupted with a sarcastic comment. "You mean poison gas, don't you?"

"Yes," the SOG scientist admitted with a nervous smile. "The gas was designed to dissipate within hours after release. Underwater, we're not sure."

"What's your best guess?"

"A week at the most."

Hiram Wilson pushed his chair back and got to his feet.

"Let's hope and pray that the ship did sink, gentlemen." He turned to Dr. Weinfield. "And that your people are right about the short life span. Otherwise we may be looking down the barrel at the possible end of civilization as we know it."

The others gathered up their papers and stood.

"One more thing," Wilson added. "If there is any leak about this to the press, the three of you will be sent to the Central Pacific to personally take charge of the search. Understand?"

Reluctantly the other three men nodded.

KARLA HAMILTON hadn't slept much since they had returned from Thailand. Nightmares filled with dead bodies kept haunting her sleep.

She had suspected when she first met Kalidonian that he was planning something bold to force governments to cooperate in saving the world from environmental destruction.

She had smelled the biggest news story of her career at that first press conference. Now she was convinced that what the old man was planning was more than just a major story. She suspected he was prepared to somehow blackmail the world by threatening to destroy it if he didn't get his way.

Kalidonian was psychotic. She was certain of that. So were the men and women around him.

She had checked into Marco Gussman's background before coming to the press conference. He had a long history of violence. There had been no record of Dr. Nis—she suspected that wasn't his real name—but after meeting him, she was convinced he was capable of doing anything without guilt or remorse.

The others who had arrived to join him were not the usual ecological fanatics who waved protest signs outside nuclear plants or research laboratories that used animals for experiments. These were hard-faced men and women whose eyes reflected their familiarity with death and killing.

She thought she had recognized some of them.

The tall Japanese woman who called herself Yoshira. Her face had been shown on television during a news brief about a terrorist group who called themselves the Japanese Red Army. She was wanted as the suspected assassin of the head of one of Japan's largest computer companies.

Or the bearded man from Turkey who claimed he was a biologist. Karla had seen pictures of him in a police lineup in Ankara. He was suspected of belonging to the Gray Wolves, a terrorist organization that attempted to kill the Pope.

As she studied the arrivals, she was convinced that these weren't environmental activists coming to Gaia to help save the world. These were experienced terrorists from every part of the world, gathering here for…she didn't know what. At least not yet.

She had photographed the faces of the men and women who had arrived—she hadn't dared use her video camera—with her spy-sized Minox. And anything else she thought might be useful, including the map on which Marco had circled major cities—and his handwritten list of certain places in each city.

She wasn't sure what the map or list meant, but she was certain they had something to do with the coming event masterminded by Kalidonian.

All she knew was that in less than thirty days, something earth-shattering—she shuddered at her choice of words—would happen.

She began to search her mind for a way to escape the biosphere-prison so she could alert the outside world. She knitted her brows as she developed and discarded a dozen scenarios before she gave up for the time being.

She had been intent on getting the scoop of her life, but now her conscience wouldn't let her rest. There was no way she could stand idly by and watch Kalidonian and his followers turn some nightmare into a hideous reality without trying to do something to stop him.

She paled as she realized that her new determination might endanger her life. Closing her eyes, she steeled herself for the task at hand.

NIS SAT in his spacious office in the biosphere and began to make a list of the places in both worlds where the missiles should be placed. He would turn over the hit list for Earth to Marco when he was done.

A visitor interrupted his work, and he looked up.

Kalidonian entered, accompanied by the man who served as his bodyguard.

"We've run into a problem," Kalidonian said hesitantly.

Nis looked surprised. "What kind of problem?"

"The aborigine natives who live in this area have surrounded Gaia. They are sitting in a large circle, chanting prayers and refusing to leave. Marco took some of our men outside the dome to threaten them. But they wouldn't leave, even after the men pointed guns at them."

"They can do nothing to stop our plans."

"They've threatened to contact the press. The area will be swarming with reporters and television people. One of them may find out something by accident."

"Maybe Karla could broadcast something that would discourage them from coming here," Marco suggested.

"No, no," the older man protested. "She should be saved for something more important like my proclamation next month."

Nis smiled. "What would you like me to do?"

"Make them go away. They'll spoil everything."

"No, they won't," Nis reassured him.

The means toward accomplishing their ends were almost at hand. They were ready to receive shipment of their powerful weapon—a freighterful of pirated gas. There was more than enough of the stuff to eliminate the nuisance outside—and it was almost time to let the inhabitants of this world know the doom they faced.

9

Twilight had fallen, and the two warriors were still riding hard in the direction of the village where Mondlock the Knower was waiting.

Hogan spoke up after a lengthy silence. "Maybe we should go after Peytok."

"My troops can handle whatever he's brought with him," Brom replied proudly. "And Mondlock made it clear that the meeting was urgent."

"Yeah, I know," the American muttered.

Brom glanced at him. "I am surprised," he admitted. "This—what was the word you used?—slimy little tyrant is a coward. Where did he find the courage to invade Kalabria?"

An uncomfortable thought had been nagging at Black Jack ever since they left the site of the attack.

"What if somebody's backing him?"

"Who would want to?"

"Remember the alien?"

They had fought a huge battle with the creature who wore the face and body of a human, and they had destroyed the force he had gathered to help him.

"We defeated him," Brom reminded Hogan.

"No, he just disappeared when we destroyed his army."

"What is there in Kalabria that he would want so badly?"

Hogan shook his head. "I don't know. But whatever it is, he's tried to find it in my world, too. Maybe Mondlock will know."

"Mondlock knows everything," the Kalabrian assured him.

Black Jack smiled. Brom sounded just as he did when describing Mok Seng.

They continued riding quietly, pushing their horses on. Suddenly Hogan stopped.

Brom called back to him. "Is something wrong?"

Hogan waited until his companion trotted over to his side. "I just remembered. We were interrupted before you answered my question."

"Question?" Brom hesitated, then donned a mask of innocence. "What question was that?"

"About what's got you so uptight?"

"Another time," the Kalabrian replied, and started to spur his mount.

"No," Hogan insisted. "Now."

The Kalabrian leader turned away and stared at the sky. Finally his haughty posture began to melt, and he faced Hogan.

"I asked Mora to go through the ceremonies of marriage with me," he said quietly.

"So what has that got to do with Mondlock?"

"Nothing," Brom admitted sheepishly.

Hogan grinned. He had known from the first time he had seen Mora and Brom together that it was only a matter of time before they formalized a relationship that had started when they were children.

"Congratulations," he said with a flash of teeth.

The Kalabrian didn't return the smile. "Thank you."

"C'mon. You knew it would happen sooner or later."

Brom looked up at the myriad of gleaming stars that were becoming visible in the sky. "My lovely Mora, I'd swear she is the same—she feels just like she used to in my arms—and yet she changed. Already she plans the ceremonies. State dinners. Festivals. Celebrations. She and Astrah have been locked behind closed doors selecting the fabrics for her ceremonial gown."

"That's what women do when they plan a wedding."

"She is also selecting the fabric for the garments *I* will wear so they will match hers."

Black Jack howled with laughter, then quickly stifled it as Brom's figure stiffened in the saddle.

"This occasion is really for women, you know, and it's only for a few days," Hogan reassured him. "Indulge her, my friend."

"It already seems like a lifetime." He shook his head. "Come. Mondlock waits for us."

Hogan remounted his animal and followed Brom along the narrow road. The Kalabrian stopped and turned back to his friend.

"What if she will make a fuss when I have to go off to battle?"

"That doesn't sound like Mora."

"But I hear women do strange things after they marry."

Trying to distract Brom from his fears, Hogan asked, "Who is standing with Mora at the ceremony?"

"Astrah, naturally."

The two women had been like sisters ever since Brom's bride-to-be had invited the former temple maiden to join the select troupe of dance warriors that Mora led.

"Don't forget to send me an invitation," Hogan commented.

"Invitation?" Brom sounded puzzled. "Why do you need an invitation when you are part of the ceremonies?"

"Me? Doing what?"

"Standing with me before the high priest."

Hogan felt honored. "Sounds like something I can handle."

It was Brom's turn to grin.

"Of course it is expected that you will have a pair of fast steeds ready outside for our escape in the event I change my mind."

Hogan thought of the wrath he would have to face if the Kalabrian did try to leave the ceremonies prematurely—not only from Brom's furious bride but from Astrah—and the rest of the women who became very intent at such events.

"That's not a wise thing to do, even for a powerful warrior. Women may be sweet and loving, but when they get wrathful, they are worse than fifty demons."

Hogan could just make out the wicked gleam that sneaked across Brom's eyes. "Of course, if I wasn't the only one going through the ordeal..." He paused. "The temple maiden and you will be at the altar anyway."

Black Jack spurred his horse and raced away. "Let's get going," he shouted over his shoulder, "and find out what's bothering Mondlock."

Brom let out a roar of a laugh and urged his steed to catch up, much pleased that he wasn't the only one feeling discomfort.

MONDLOCK HUDDLED in front of the fire and stared into the flames. He had pulled his heavy gray robe around him as if he were still cold despite the heat from the burning logs.

Brom and Hogan sat silently and waited for him to speak. They knew that there was no way to get the wise man to talk until he was ready.

"Why did you want us to meet you here?"

Mondlock leaned closer to the fire, seeking its warmth. His long, thin face was covered with the wrinkles of age, and his dark hair was sprinkled with gray. Yet he didn't look old. His deep-set sapphire eyes burned brightly with the fire of a younger man.

Many years before he had come out of the west and across the mountains of the gods from the legendary city of Leanad—where students were taught the secrets of the Know—to become chief counselor to Brom's father, and now to Brom.

"A passing farmer found this place and in terror rode all night to Tella to tell me what he had seen."

Weariness etched the wise man's saddened face.

"Perhaps not even Ost can save our world from its doom," he continued in a low voice.

Brom was the first to ask, "What happened?"

Mondlock rose to his feet and vanished into the dark. Soon he returned, carrying a small object wrapped in a blanket. Gently he set it on the ground.

"I will show you," he said sadly.

Reaching down, he pulled the blanket away and exposed the body of a small child. It pained all of them to see the obvious suffering of the child's passing.

Stunned, Brom asked the obvious question.

"What caused this death?"

Mondlock shook his head. "I do not know. If this is an illness, I have never seen it before."

The Kalabrian ruler felt a deep pang of concern. If Mondlock didn't know, no one knew. Mondlock was the wisest of all the Knowers in the world. Ambassadors from faraway lands had come to plead with Brom to allow them to spend an hour or two with Mondlock so they could carry back with them some of his knowledge.

"There were horrible sores on the child's face and body. And on the faces and bodies of the others," he added.

Hogan stared angrily at the tiny body. "How many others?"

The wise man pointed to the dark. "Once there was a village just past the hills." He turned to Brom. "It was a small place, but twenty-three families lived here. A hundred and twenty-four people—men, women and children.''

Brom tried unsuccessfully to pierce the dark with his eyes.

''Where are they?''

''Dead. Every one of them.''

Hogan remembered photographs of villages in the Middle East of his world. An insane dictator had decided to test the quality of the poison gas he was manufacturing on one of the minorities in the country he ruled.

There were sores on those bodies. And something else.

Signs that something had stopped their breathing.

''Were there any signs they couldn't breathe?''

Mondlock nodded his head. ''Many of them clutched at their throats as they were struggling against some invisible demon who had come to suck life from them.''

Who could have such powers? Hogan wondered, then a face suddenly appeared in his mind's eye. Flawless features, blond hair, Oriental eyes...but somebody who seemed to have no material substance. A creature from God knew where, from the uncharted reaches of the universe.

''Nis,'' he said quietly.

The two warriors stared at one another. They remembered the creature who called himself Nis and his previous attempts at conquering Kalabria.

Brom spoke first. ''The strange being from another world?''

Hogan shrugged. ''But why would he want to kill a village of farmers?''

Brom nodded. ''And with what?''

Mondlock waited for them to finish their exchange. ''The secret of Ost has not yet been discovered,'' he told them. ''That is what this creature seeks.''

Hogan turned to him. ''What is the secret of Ost?''

"All of our gods are powerful," Mondlock replied evasively.

The American could recite the list of gods whom the Kalabrians worshiped.

Ost had created the universe, according to the Kalabrians. Sundra, the Sky Father, and his mate, Hudha, the Earth Mother, lived in a palace in the remote Anatak Mountains, which rose west of the unpassable desert called the Forbidden Region.

Terina, the Earth Mother's daughter, took care of making the grass and plants grow. Her brother, Morok, made sure the land had enough rain or snow, according to the season. Sena dispensed wisdom and knowledge while his sister, Wassa, grew the special plants and herbs used by the priests to keep the Kalabrians well. Her daughter, Lusana, concerned herself with beauty, love and passion. Pavad was the receiver of the dead. It was he who escorted the bodies of Kalabrian warriors to their eternal resting places on the ledges below the home of the gods on Mount Anatak.

Dozens of smaller gods were assigned by Sundra or Hudha to a specific task.

At one time, on Hogan's early journeys to Kalabria, Brom and his people had even considered him to be one of their gods—the god of war and vengeance, Komar.

Hogan was not one to believe in gods. He sounded cynical when he asked, "With so many gods, why worry about Ost?"

"Ost is the most powerful of them all. It was his energy that formed the universe and created this world. Without Ost we would cease existing."

Black Jack wasn't interested in a lecture on religion. Impatient, he asked, "What's that got to do with the weird alien?"

"When he stole the medallion of Ost that I wore—and the similar medallions from the other priests whom he had destroyed—I began to understand that he had come to this world to rob us of Ost's power."

Hogan was getting confused. "What's this power you talk about?"

"Each of the medallions contained a bit of Ost in them. Enough to temporarily satisfy whatever hunger the creature had. He had returned to find the rest of Ost."

Brom stared at the elderly man. "This power you speak of—does it exist in some physical form?"

Mondlock nodded. "There is a temple in which Ost lives. It is well hidden so that a casual traveler would not come upon it accidentally. Even someone seeking it couldn't discover its location unless he was led to it. This is what the creature you call Nis seeks."

"We don't really know that he's back," Hogan reminded him.

The Knower smiled sadly. "He is back. Look at the bodies in the village and you will see what he plans to do to the rest of our world." He paused. "And perhaps to your world, as well."

Hogan glanced at the sore-riddled body of the small child. The rage inside him was building as he thought of the helpless youngster whose future had been stolen.

"If he is here, we shall find and destroy him," Brom growled.

"He has the killing wind," Mondlock replied in a flat tone.

Hogan got to his feet and walked to where the wise man had set down the body. Reaching into his musette bag, he searched for the small medical kit he knew was there.

There was a syringe in it. Hogan inserted the needle into a vein on the forearm of the dead child and withdrew blood.

Brom looked at him in shock. "What are you doing?"

"Trying to find out what killed these people, and if there's a way to stop it."

He rose to his feet. He had to return to his own world. The joy of being with Astrah would have to wait for his return. He didn't know if he would be successful, but he closed his eyes, summoning up vivid images of Earth. When he opened them again, the shimmering cloud appeared. He gathered up his weapons and walked toward it.

"Wait, Hogan. You are needed here," Brom called out.

"Let him go," Mondlock said, laying a hand on his arm. "It is impossible for even you two to do battle with invisible air. And perhaps in his world he can find a solution."

If Hogan couldn't, there was no hope for either of the worlds.

10

Argun Kalidonian strolled past the administrative buildings while his entourage trailed along just behind him.

He was back in Gaia, surrounded by the dream that had kept him alive since his son's death.

It was the ideal environment in which to start the new civilization that would soon replace the imperfect one that had spent thousands of years destroying people and the planet.

He was impatient to get going. He looked up at the transparent shell of reinforced glass that separated the enclosed city named after the Earth Goddess of Greek mythology from the hostile Australian outback.

To think that so thin a material would protect his carefully built world from the death that would soon erase all the human predators.

He had waited a long time to make his dream come true. The huge fortune he had built through his countless companies had been invested in this city. The companies themselves had been sold off one by one to raise the money he needed for the design and construction.

The news that he was going to construct the largest biosphere ever attempted had attracted worldwide attention. More than a dozen of the top architects competed for the contract to design the structure, and one of the three largest construction companies agreed to meet the accelerated completion timetable Kalidonian demanded.

He had taken Dr. Nis's advice and held a series of showings for the media, personally conducting the visitors around the half-mile area that would be enclosed. Using sketches and scale models, he made sure to go into infinite detail. He achieved what he had set out to do, which was to make sure that Gaia was no longer of interest to the public.

The curiosity seekers had stopped traveling across the Australian desert for a look at the giant structure, and the press hadn't contacted him for months.

As far as the outside world was concerned, he was conducting a large-scale experiment. One hundred volunteers would live inside the hemispheric structure for two years and conduct a series of tests on surviving in a climate-controlled environment.

What he didn't tell outsiders was that he was preparing the carefully selected hundred men and women to join him to help create a perfect civilization once the world outside capitulated to him—or died resisting.

He shivered with excitement as he turned to one of the two people accompanying him.

"When will we be fully functional, Marco?"

"The biosphere is already functional now, Kalidonian."

"The recirculating water supply system?"

Marco nodded. "Operational as of this morning."

"Air and power systems?"

"We can be self-sustaining at any time."

"The supplies until our plantings are mature?"

"On their way by transport helicopter."

"The recruiting?"

"The rest of the recruits should be arriving within a few days."

"You've screened them carefully?"

"Every one of them will be a valuable addition to Gaia."

What Marco did not add was that each was also a trained terrorist committed to helping him blackmail the reactionaries of the world into submission.

He turned to his second companion. Like the other two, Karla Hamilton was dressed in a simple one-piece knit jumpsuit that did nothing to hide her lissome form.

"Perhaps you should delay the start of your plan for a few weeks so the new people can be properly oriented," she suggested nervously.

But Nis had warned Gussman that the timetable he had prepared couldn't be altered.

"There will be enough time after they see what is happening outside Gaia for that," Marco commented.

"Anything else?"

"The aborigines have sent representatives to complain that we have violated our agreement with them and are desecrating their sacred lands," Marco reported.

Kalidonian brushed aside the complaint with a wave of his hand.

"They say they're going to use their magic to get their gods to destroy us if we don't move the biosphere," Marco added.

Kalidonian allowed a faint mocking smile to light his face. "Surely you're not afraid of their magic."

"What concerns me is that they're going to bring attention to us when we don't want it," Gussman growled.

Karla's eyes brightened. "Perhaps I could help. Sometimes a woman can be more convincing than a man. I could talk to them and explain how you are planning to save their lands from ecological destruction, too."

Kalidonian gave her an indulgent look. "Don't worry yourself about them, my dear child. I'm sure Marco will find a way to deal with them."

With a lighter step now, Kalidonian walked toward the structure that housed his office.

When he reached it, Alexander Nis was waiting for him in the large circular room. Nis looked pleased.

"The cargo has arrived at the warehouse."

Kalidonian was jubilant. Nis had not failed him again. Ever since the scientist had offered his services to help in achieving his goals, Nis had been his most valuable aide. He was the one who discovered that the Americans were shipping quantities of their poison gas to a remote Pacific atoll and urged him to find a way to acquire it to back up his demands.

"What about the captain and his men?"

"All hands were lost at sea."

Kalidonian's eyes became moist. "Was that necessary?"

"As you said, thirty million dollars is a lot of money. And the fewer who know our plans, the less chance there is of leaks."

That was the only thing that bothered Kalidonian about Alexander Nis. He had never felt any warmth emanating from him, nor signs of the reluctance he personally felt—but always overcame—to kill.

Kalidonian started to make his way toward the doors at the far end of the room. He turned back to Nis one last time.

"Is this the right thing I am doing?"

Nis spread his hands beseechingly. "Who will save the Earth if you don't?"

Kalidonian hesitated. He thought about the vow he had taken after his son's family and thousands of others had died because an incompetent technician had accidentally opened a discharge valve and released tons of the poisonous fumes from the plant into the atmosphere.

"Those who would destroy the Earth must themselves be destroyed. An eye for an eye," he had pledged at the gravesite of his son.

He too deserved to be punished. But perhaps his attempts to save what was left of the world would be penance enough.

He mentioned Marco Gussman's concerns about the complaining aborigines.

"I'll handle it," Nis promised.

"You are a good friend, Alexander Nis," Kalidonian said, sounding relieved.

Suddenly his voice filled with excitement. "Nothing can stop us now."

HIRAM WILSON STUDIED the sealed package sitting on his desk. Hogan had called and left a message regarding the parcel with his secretary, Mrs. Bolivar.

He looked up at her inquiringly. "Did he say what was in it?"

"A syringe full of blood from the body of a dead child," she replied, reading from her shorthand notes.

"What does he want me to do with it?"

"Have it tested."

"For what?"

"He wouldn't say," Mrs. Bolivar replied. "He would only say that if he was right, you'd know why he sent it."

Wilson knew about Hogan's dedication to the welfare of small children. Hogan contributed most of the fees he received from the American government to various children's charities.

"Where was he calling from?"

"Don Muang Airport in Bangkok."

"What the hell was he doing there?"

"I asked him that very same question," the secretary said, then added, "though not quite the same way."

Wilson was impatient. "Just what did he say?"

"He said he was hitching a ride up north."

Wilson started to ask why Hogan would be heading in that direction, then realized his secretary wouldn't know.

As if she had read his mind, she added, "When I asked him why he was going up north, he hung up."

Wilson sighed in frustration. "Get this over to the National Institute of Health lab and have them call me the minute they finish analyzing it," he said, handing her the small sealed package.

"And tell them to handle it carefully. Who knows what kind of disease it contains."

THE THAI ARMY helicopter pilot was puzzled. His orders were to fly the American passenger to whatever location he wanted.

"You are sure this is where you want me to leave you? There is nothing here but poor villages and mountains."

Black Jack nodded. "Yeah, this is the spot. Just drop me off here."

Captain Sarit Yontrakit wondered why the American, dressed in denim jeans, work shirt and black cowboy boots, was exploring the hilly world of the Lahu tribes. Perhaps he was somehow involved in the opium trade. The infamous Golden Triangle, where Burma and Laos met with Thailand, was not far away. It was from this area that much of the world's supply of opium originated.

The Lahu tribes, who helped cultivate the poppies, then picked and transported the harvest to hidden laboratories tucked among the mountains, were an essential part of the opium chain.

The captain was tempted to draw his passenger out on the subject, except for his forbidding expression. There was something about the way the man carried himself that was reminiscent of a cobra—coiled and ready to strike at the first sign of any sudden move against him.

Captain Yontrakit watched as the strange American climbed out of the whirlybird, adjusted his backpack and wandered down the road to Chiang Rai.

He had seen the tall man enter the air base, located outside of Bangkok, and go into the office of the base commander, and wondered who he was.

Someone important, he had decided when an aide to the commander came out with the American and ordered him to fly the man to any destination he chose.

As he started the blades of his helicopter spinning, Sarit Yontrakit wondered just who in Bangkok would be interested in knowing the movements of the American.

For a fee, naturally. Everything he wanted to buy had become too expensive to afford on just his military pay.

IT HAD BEEN a long time since Hogan had been in the area. More than sixteen years.

The armored trucks were gone. So were the huge mounds of supplies, and the soldiers and the mercenaries who had used the region as a base of operations from which they launched attacks under his leadership across the Mekong River into Vietnam.

But everything else was the same, including the steady rain of this season and the unpaved roads.

He stopped and checked the map he had taken from the body of the dead Vietnamese terrorist. This was the area that had been circled. As he continued to walk along the soggy dirt road, he tried to figure out just what was the professional killer's interest in the area.

Ahead of him a village of Lahu families from someplace in the west was on the move. The male heads carried the worldly possessions of the families on their backs, while the women drove the livestock—a pair of pigs for breeding—

along the road. The children carried baskets with chickens in them.

A few ponies lumbered behind, toting the village's anvil and blacksmithing tools.

Hogan tried to avoid staring at the villagers. Especially the younger women. But, as he kept reminding himself, he was only human, and none of the women wore anything except a black silk sarong as they paraded proudly along the road. Despite the rain, they smiled as they looked back and saw him looking after them.

Hogan stopped and wouldn't move until the villagers disappeared into the thick, wet foliage that led to the foothills of the nearby mountain range. Then he turned and proceeded toward the village of Chiang Rai.

THE THAI POLICE OFFICER was expecting him. He stood outside the small building that served as the area's law enforcement center and leaned on an ancient jeep seemingly oblivious to the steady rain that had drenched his tan uniform.

Black Jack recognized him right away. Ca Co Maw had been his chief guide during the war.

The policeman studied the expression on the American's face.

"You look like you've seen a demon or an evil spirit," he commented.

"No, I saw the delightful girls from one of the villages walking along the road," Hogan replied. "I thought most of the tribes had been converted by missionaries."

"That didn't change how they dressed," the Thai policeman replied pleasantly. "For many here, converting to the Western religion only changed what spirits and demons they believed in."

"I just forgot how beautiful the Lahu women are."

"Or how angry their menfolk can get if they are tampered with," the policeman said with a smile. "But come inside."

The one-room hut was simply furnished with a desk, a telephone, a cot and small propane gas stove. Light came through the window from outside during the day, and in the evening from a single naked bulb in the plain ceiling fixture.

Hanging from nails in the wall were changes of clothes. There was no bathroom. Like the villagers, Ca Co Maw had dug a hole behind the police hut, where he could relieve himself.

"I see you still don't have a sink, bathtub or a shower," Black Jack commented.

The Thai officer opened the door, then stuck a metal cup out in the rain. The sound of heavy drops bouncing around inside the vessel echoed as he turned to the American.

"Who needs a sink or shower when I have clean rain to cook with or to wash my body and clothes?"

Hogan grinned. "When was the last time you did either, old friend?"

Ca Co Maw looked down at his rumpled uniform. "I suppose it is time to do both."

The American laughed and slapped the other's back.

"Not on my behalf. You are not my type, Ca Co Maw."

"For which I am eternally grateful," the Thai replied as he fished a bottle of Mekong brandy from a desk drawer.

Filling two metal cups with the tan-colored liquor, he handed one to Hogan, then took a sip from his own.

"You should have been wiser and not come back, Hogan."

Hogan had tasted the powerful liquor before. Cautiously he sipped a thimbleful. Already he could feel his insides peeling as the drops of locally produced drink touched them.

Inhaling air to cool his stomach, he asked, "Because of the village women?"

"I was not referring to them," Ca Co Maw replied obliquely.

"Many years ago you told me that this would always be my home if I wanted to live here."

"That was in another life. Times were different. You were a different person."

Hogan understood that something was wrong. "Have I changed so much?"

"Perhaps not. But others have."

Hogan didn't have time to tiptoe around.

"Who are the others?"

"The hills are no longer the innocent haven of hunters of the mighty sambar stag and the growers of the white flowers."

Black Jack knew all about the region's dependency on growing the poppy that was the basis for opium.

"Have the drug wars come to the hill country?"

"Even worse. The political killers have descended on us."

"Do you mean government agents from Bangkok?"

"No. Two carloads of men arrived here within the week. Strangers from the other side of the Mekong River."

Hogan nodded grimly. Vietnam was on the other side of the Mekong.

"They brought death with them," the Thai added.

"Whose death?"

"They released a vapor from a canister they carried. An entire village died."

An alarm went off in Hogan's head. The warnings from Mok Seng and Mondlock. The village in Kalabria. Now this village. He desperately wanted to interrogate the killers.

"Did you capture them?"

"No. They had disappeared before the bodies of the villagers were found."

Hogan's face became grim. "I want to see this village of the dead."

He slipped his backpack off, then leaned down and opened it. From inside he slipped out his gun belt and buckled it around his waist. The 9 mm Beretta was in the holster that hung from the leather.

From a canvas roll, he retrieved the eighteen-inch knife and eased it into its scabbard. Then he took out a 9 mm Uzi pistol and snapped in a 30-round clip.

"There is no point. Other villagers buried the bodies. They were afraid the death was contagious. The bodies were covered with sores."

"I will go anyway to see if I can learn what killed the villagers. Then I can find the others who are responsible and punish them."

Ca Co Maw's voice became softer. "Don't go, old friend. The village is in the Fang Plain, at the foot of the 'Mountain City of Cliffs' where a host of demons and evil spirits wait to claim the souls of unwise travelers who venture there."

Hogan had seen the so-called city from a helicopter many years ago. As he remembered, the "Mountain City" was a wall of cliffs that rose six thousand feet and closed in the verdant valley. From the top of the cliffs, the borders of Burma to the north and Laos to the east could be seen.

He recalled a Buddhist proverb the Cambodian abbot had quoted as part of one of his lessons.

"To be blind to the wicked is the beginning of wickedness," he told the Thai policeman.

"Yes," the Thai replied, then, with a sad smile, asked, "What is it you want from me, old friend?"

"Somebody who'll rent me a car or drive me to the village."

Ca Co Maw sighed in resignation.

"Drive my jeep there if you are foolish, Hogan."

"What happens to your jeep if I am killed?"

Ca Co Maw nodded. "Somebody will drive it back to me."

The two men embraced. Then Black Jack dropped his weapons and backpack on the passenger seat and climbed in behind the steering wheel.

Ca Co Maw put a hand on the steering wheel. "There is something else you should know. The canister that contained the death was found by the villagers. The words painted on it said that what was in it was manufactured by your country."

Black Jack was stunned. This was bad—not even bad but scary news. He had to see it for himself, though.

"Before you leave," the policeman added, "I should tell you there are those among the Lahu who would punish those who made the death material, as well as those who released it."

Hogan understood the risk, but the information he might gain from the journey was worth it.

As he drove away, Hogan knew the tribesmen would be expecting him. Somehow—he didn't know how—the Thai police officer would get a message to the hill tribes that he was on his way.

And hopefully along with it would go a plea to let him live so he could avenge the deaths of the villagers.

11

There was a thick carpet of stars in the sky overhead. Shivering in the chill of the red sand country night, Stanley Bartlett leaned against the fender of the truck and took a pack of Rothmans out of a pocket of his worn safari jacket. He started to light it when the tall, skinny man inside the cab of the vehicle snapped a warning.

"Put that thing out. You want the bloody 'abos' to know we're here, Stanley?"

Defiantly the stocky unshaven man flicked his lighter and held the bright flame to the end of his cigarette.

"Hell, the bloody abos know we're here. Them black savages know everything. Did you hear the sticks clicking and the funny horn moaning in the dark when we drove in? This place gives me the creeps, Reggie."

Both of them had heard the deep tones of the didgeridoo, the wind instrument made from an eight-foot hollowed tree, as they rode along the private road. It had been whistling its deep, moaning sound ever since.

"Bloody aborigines are trying to scare us away," the thin man replied. "Bunch of mumbo jumbo, that's what it is."

"What about them dingoes howling their heads off, like they were signaling each other to get ready to attack us?"

The skinny man patted the M-16A rifle he had slung on his shoulder. "Them wild dogs will change their mind after I knock off a couple of them with this," he bragged. Then he snapped an order. "Let's get the launcher hooked up. After that it won't matter if the aborigines know that we're here."

The tall man got out of the truck and moved to the canvas-covered object mounted on the flatbed.

"Let's get busy," Reggie Tomasino snapped as he began to untie the tarpaulin. "Even being close to these damn abos with their hocus-pocus gives me the willies," he admitted.

Like Bartlett, Tomasino has been born and raised in the slums of Sydney. Being in the desertlike heart of the outback among the Pitjantjatjara aborigines and their chanting Marngit priests, who acted like medicine men, made him edgy.

If it weren't for the money he was being paid for this job, Tomasino would have left the day he'd landed in Alice Springs, the only large community for a thousand miles. But the swarthy character who called himself Marco was paying more than Reggie Tomasino had ever received on a job.

Just to launch a small bomb at a bunch of savages.

Easiest money he had ever made, Reggie reminded himself as he looked around to make sure there were none of the poisonous snakes he heard about nearby. Then he turned and walked to the rear of the flatbed truck.

Bartlett didn't lift a hand to help him as he revealed the small missile launcher he had mounted on the back.

"Hey," Tomasino snapped angrily. "You want your share of the money, you move your ass and give me a bloody hand before the abos decide to come around and find out what we're doing here."

The stocky man dropped his cigarette and ground it under his boot.

"Don't get uppity, mate," he muttered. "I didn't sign on as a laborer, y'know. You hired me to launch the damn bomb, not carry it."

He watched Tomasino struggle to lift the large shell by himself, then grumbled as he walked over to help.

"Take it easy, mate. Them abos ain't goin' anywhere—except to wherever their medicine men call heaven."

To get to this point in the plan, they had waited for night before they had left Alice Springs and driven the Stuart Highway west to where it connected with the Petermann road.

They drove along the edge of the Uluru Nation Park, where the Ayers Rock—the largest isolated rock in the world—rose 1100 feet above the plains, until they reached the private road that led to the strange domed structure that rose like a half balloon from the desertlike floor of the outback—as the locals called this part of the Northern Territories.

Without saying it, the two men knew that there was something strange about the place. Even more strange than the half round in which the German character and his mates lived.

Even though they couldn't see the natives who lived in the region, they could sense their presence.

Stanley Bartlett had propped his 9 mm Heckler & Koch Model HK 94-42 automatic rifle on his opened truck window, ready to fire the fifteen rounds of soft-nosed shells in the clip.

Suddenly the hemisphere-shaped structure had loomed up before them.

Bartlett had gasped. "What the hell's that?"

"That German called it a biosphere. Some kind of scientific experiment he and his mates are conducting in the outback."

"Looks like a bloody spaceship," the stocky man had mumbled.

"Got the abos all shook up, too. According to this Gussman fellow, they've been threatening to put together an army and kill everybody inside that thing as punishment for trespassing on their sacred land."

"From what I hear, the bloody abos think everything in Australia is sacred land. Good thing we're getting rid of them before they try to take the whole country back."

"Not after tonight they won't."

The truck had kept moving. In the dark they had seen vague shadows scurrying back and forth and heard the sound of the didgeridoo horn.

The stocky man had tightened his grip on his automatic rifle.

"Think they'll attack the truck?"

"From what I hear, that's not how the bloody abos operate. They'll try to scare us to death with the black magic. Like they've been trying to do to the folks inside that biosphere."

The didgeridoo sounded louder now, increasing their unease. They had wasted enough time talking, Tomasino decided. It was time to do their job and get out of the region before they tangled with the local authorities.

He opened the door of the cab of the truck. Without turning around, he called out over his shoulder.

"Come on and give us a hand with this thing."

The stocky man joined him and stared at the shiny metal shell that sat on the floor of the cab behind the driver's seat.

"Hard to believe something that small can kill everything for five miles around."

"Believe it, mate," Tomasino said. Then added, "Let's get them damn coveralls that German character gave us on so we don't end up like the abos."

From a large canvas bag, he took out two thin metallic-looking coveralls. He handed one to Bartlett, and they slipped into the lightweight contamination suits.

"Look," Bartlett laughed, waving his hands in the air. "Damn things even got mittens and booties like what a tyke would wear in winter."

Bartlett reached back inside the truck and took out two gas masks. Both men pulled the hooded shields over their heads and sealed them to their coveralls with the attached Velcro strips.

"It's going to get hot as hell in here," Bartlett complained in a voice muffled by the hood.

"Not as hot as it's going to get for the abos," Tomasino replied. He reached down and started to slide the metal missile out of the truck cab.

"Easy with that, mate," Bartlett snapped. "You want the damn gas in there to hit us?"

"That's why we're wearing these damn outfits. So we're protected."

"Yeah, but why take chances," the stocky man muttered as he helped carry the metal shell to the back of the truck.

Together they climbed onto the truck and set the cylinder on the launcher.

For a moment Bartlett fiddled with the various controls, then called out, "Feels like I'm back in the bloody army," he cracked.

"Stop talking and let's get this thing launched. I just want to get out of here and collect our money."

Bartlett made some final adjustments. "Ready," he announced, then stopped and turned to Tomasino. "Notice anything?"

"Only that the dingoes are howling, that damn abo horn is driving me nuts and you're talking instead of doing your job."

"No. Notice these suits don't get hot."

"Probably got some kind of one-way vents built into them," Tomasino muttered. "What's the diff, Bartlett? We ain't going to be wearing them for long."

THE GLARE of the cottonwood tree fire danced across the painted faces. In a slow steady rhythm each of the several hundred men seated on the ground facing the flames clapped their spirit sticks.

"It is time for the red ochre man to come;" the oldest of them said loudly.

From out of the darkness came a small figure covered in red ochre clay, wearing the symbols of his authority.

To those men assembled, this was the ultimate authority, the judge who could decide the fate of wrongdoers, settle disputes and even command the members of the tribe to go to war, without having to seek approval.

As the red ochre man moved around the fire, stopping to ask questions of one of the elders, then moving to another with more questions, Tommy Makkarouba wondered why the elders had called for a corroboree—a gathering of the tribe.

His father was one of the elders. He wouldn't say why it was so important that Tommy leave his graduate studies at the Northern Territories University in Darwin to come home to participate in the ceremonies.

He wondered which of the ranchers who ran cattle stations in the outback had violated the sacred ground since the last gathering when it had been agreed that the buildings of a white rancher, who had desecrated one of the Songline paths of their ancestors that crisscrossed the outback, should be burnt down. And his foreman, a member of the Yankunjatjara tribe, who had encouraged him to ignore the warnings of the tribal elders, should be turned over to the

Kaditja man—the traveling executioner of the aborigines—for appropriate punishment.

Afterward the Australian government officials had promised to enforce the law that protected their lands.

The Pitjantjatjara and the land had been here since the Dreamtime, when the singing spirits created the world and all of the species that lived with it. As they crossed the lands, the ancient ones left Songlines—trails marked with symbols of one of their many gods—as memories of their passages.

Strangers had come from across the great waters to steal the soul of the land. Already they had taken over the lands near the waters. Now they were moving inland. Not just the few who built cattle or sheep stations, but those who were erecting strange structures.

Like Argun Kalidonian, the retired industrialist, who had built a giant bubble in the middle of the desert in which he announced he would create the model of an ecologically perfect world.

Tommy Makkarouba knew a lot about the biosphere. He had hired out as a construction worker on the structure to accumulate money for college.

Privately he believed the wealthy environmentalist was on the right track. The world was too busy to worry about such things as acid rain, pollution, the destruction of rain forests and other natural treasures. Somebody had to make them aware of the doomsday that would be coming soon if they didn't open their eyes.

He couldn't say such things here. No, his father and the other elders were too intent on revenge to listen to him.

He heard the voice of the red ochre man.

"Here is my decision," the clay-covered figure said loudly. "This thing that looms before us." He pointed to the biosphere in the distance. "As caretakers of this land, we must destroy it. And punish those inside for creating it on lands sacred to our ancestors.''

The young graduate student was tempted to jump to his feet and protest. He knew that the aborigine tribes viewed themselves as protectors of the lands they occupied, rather than owners. But they had no right to take the lives of others.

Before he could say anything, the tribal judge continued.

''To do this, we shall call on Wanambi, the rainbow serpent, and Bulari, the great mother, to emit a cloud of *arukwita*—the essence of death and destruction—on their trespassers. We shall summon from Bralgu—the place of the dead—the malevolent spirits—the *wardu*—to destroy the white man, the accursed *balanda,* and his monstrous house. We shall drum and dance and chant until this had happened and the evil ones inside are dead.''

The young graduate student sighed. What the red ochre man had decided was that he, like the other Pitjantjatjara, would sit here for days—or until the red ochre man saved face by announcing that the white men were spiritually dead and he could return to Darwin.

Resigned to the fact that he would be stuck here for God knew how long, Tommy Makkarouba uncrossed his legs and tried to relieve his knotted muscles.

STANLEY BARTLETT fussed over the controls.

''Come on, mate,'' Tomasino growled, clenching his M-16A nervously as he tried to pierce the dark with his eyes. ''Let's get it over with before them damn abos decide to come around to see what we're up to.''

''Got to get this thing aimed just right. How far away do you think they are?''

''Don't matter a damn, mate. It'll kill everything for miles.''

"All right," Bartlett said. "Here goes."

With a gentle pressure on the release mechanism, he watched the silvery cylinder leave the launcher in a burst of controlled fire and spiral elegantly through the air like a well-thrown football.

"Let's get out of here," Tomasino said, jumping down from the back of the truck.

WITH A SOFT HUSH the shell crashed into an outcropping of sandstone boulders. The only sound was the hiss from the escaping gas.

Slowly the invisible vapor moved across the land and reached the gathering of Pitjantjatjara.

Suddenly the red ochre man stared into space.

"Now the land will die and so will we," the tribal judge said quietly.

Tommy wondered what provoked the dire prediction. He looked around and realized two of the others sitting around the fire had slumped forward. He turned to his father and saw him fall backward.

Then he felt the searing pain as something invisible burned into his eyes, his nostrils, his mouth. He tore at his face, trying to pull off whatever demon it was that tried to possess him, then fell forward, dead.

BARTLETT AND TOMASINO sat up in the cab of the truck, still in their contamination suits. The tall, skinny man had one hand frozen on the wheel. The other was on the key in the ignition, where it would stay until somebody found their bodies, clad in the thin, metallic contamination uniforms that contained minuscule slits around the face and chest areas.

12

Hogan drove slowly as he approached Doi Vieng Pha, the sharp ridge that separated the people of the Fang Plain from their more savage countrymen who lived in the upland hills of northern Thailand.

Even from this distance the top of the mountain looked like the dwelling for demons. Shrouded in the gloomy clouds and damp mists of the long rainy season, Doi Vieng was a forbidding sight.

From the valley the American could see the dark forests of wind-tortured trees and hear the wailing winds that raced across the mountain's jagged rocks.

Like the sound of Brom's howling sword, Black Jack told himself.

As he moved forward on the unpaved road, he could hear the whooping of families of gibbon apes and the distant roars of tigers searching the thick forests for their meals.

His right hand grasped the 9 mm Uzi automatic pistol as he steered with his left. He was ready for a surprise attack from an animal or human.

It came as he eased around a bend and saw the thick trunk of a large teak blocking the road.

Accident or ambush? he wondered.

He got his answer moments later when three wiry Lahu hunters jumped from behind the foliage that crowded the edges of the narrow road and aimed their Vietnam War vintage M16s at him.

Easing his grip on his automatic, Black Jack stopped the jeep and waited for the three to approach.

The ambushers studied the vehicle from a distance, then talked among themselves in low voices. Finally one of them, a thick-necked man with a wide scar on his right temple, cautiously approached Hogan.

"You are American?"

When Hogan nodded, the man stared at him with suspicion.

"How come you to this car? It belongs to Ca Co Maw, the policeman."

Black Jack held back his smile. He had been through many similar interrogations when he had trained his men here during the war.

"He lent it to me."

"Why would the policeman do such a thing?"

"Because we are friends."

"Ca Co Maw has no American friends."

The American agent saw that the others nodded in agreement as they tightened their grip on their weapons.

He knew he didn't have much time to convince the men he had come here for peaceful reasons. The Lahu tribesmen were not a patient people, as he remembered.

Hogan kept his hand near the trigger housing of his automatic weapon. He hoped he wouldn't have to shoot his way out of the valley.

"We were together during the war. He worked for me."

The explanation brought a new round of whispering among the men. Black Jack began to calculate the chances of his hitting all three with rounds from his Uzi before they killed him.

The whispered conference ended, and the man who had interrogated him brought another to the jeep.

Hogan studied the new face. The Lahu tribesman was old. Probably over forty, Black Jack thought. A venerable age in the lifespan of the hill people.

In turn, the wrinkled face stared at him coldly, then broke into a toothless smile.

"You are Hogan," the wrinkled face said.

The American relaxed and let his breath out.

"Yes, I am Hogan. Who are you?"

"I am called Pig Killer," the tribesman replied proudly. "You and your men lived in my village."

Hogan recalled the tradition of Lahu tribesmen taking nicknames that described their hunting skills. He had learned such things during the several months he had spent in the Fang Plain. They were there, he remembered reminding his team, to conduct missions against the North Vietnamese Army. Not to violate the honor of the hill people.

Only one of his men had, and Black Jack had shipped him back to his infantry unit an hour after he caught him making love to a villager's pretty young wife.

The incident won him the increased respect of the hill people.

All the Lahu girls, as he recalled, were pretty, and seemingly willing to take on new lovers before they settled down and got married.

They especially liked Hogan, who was like a chieftain to them. But a lot of cold swims in the local rivers later, Black Jack and his men had departed the valley, frustrated and celibate, taking with them several of the younger tribesmen who had volunteered to serve as scouts.

"This is Stud Bull," the man who called himself Pig Killer said, giggling as he pointed to the first man who had spoken to Black Jack. "He has four wives and seventeen children," he added by way of explanation. "The other man is Little Pig Killer. He is one of my sons."

More relaxed, Stud Bull let his eyes wander to the weapon Hogan held loosely in his right hand.

"I have not seen so tiny a rifle," he said.

He held out a hand, and reluctantly the American handed the automatic to him.

The small, wiry man held the mini-Uzi against his shoulder and leaned his chin against the stock. Searching through the open sights, he moved the weapon across the nearby forest, then suddenly squeezed the trigger.

A long burst exploded, stunning Stud Bull and the other tribesmen. He stared at the small automatic.

"A powerful weapon," he commented with admiration.

Hogan held out a hand. For a moment Stud Bull refused to move, then slowly handed the Uzi back.

Little Pig Killer had wandered into the forest. Emerging from the thick woods, he shouted something in the Lahu tongue.

Hogan looked to Pig Killer for an explanation.

"The small gun has killed a large sambar stag," the elderly man explained happily. "Our village will eat well for many days." He turned to the others and asked a question in his native language. The other two nodded.

Pig Killer turned back to the American.

"Since you provided the means to kill this mighty animal, you will be our honored guest."

Hogan decided to ask his questions now, rather than wait until they had all eaten.

"No one has asked me why I have come here."

"To hunt and to get away from the madness of the world outside, of course," the man called Pig Killer replied. "All men must find peace for their souls, or they will be swallowed by the demons of the world."

"There is no time for that. I have come to find out why a village of Lahu was murdered."

The friendly expressions on the faces of the tribesmen vanished to be replaced by angry stares as the men once more gripped their weapons tightly.

"Perhaps you can tell us," Stud Bull said.

13

Pig Killer had dressed the stag. Now a shoulder haunch of the noble beast was cooking over a huge fire sheltered from the steady downpour of rain by an overhanging rock.

Black Jack could smell the tantalizing aroma of roasting meat, but for now he wasn't hungry.

He sat on a fallen log in the rain-drenched clearing. The other two sat on elephant's ear leaves and stared at him.

"Your country dropped many chemical from the sky," Stud Bull said as an accusation.

Hogan was in no mood to defend the actions of the United States during the war. Especially since he didn't agree with many of them.

"That was in time of war," he replied bluntly.

"Since then the Americans have become friendly with the killers of the hill people of their country," Stud Bull continued.

Black Jack remembered the secret campaign of both the North and South Vietnamese governments to eliminate the tough, independence-minded montagnards, who lived in the central highlands. Their only friends were the Special Forces troops. There was something about the determination of the proud, fierce hill tribesmen that had earned the respect of the Green Berets.

The American turned to Pig Killer, who was tearing wild greens and dropping them into a pot of boiling water.

"Pig Killer, tell these men how the Americans treated the men from the hills."

The elderly man turned around and grinned, showing his toothless gums again. "Like brothers," he called out happily.

Hogan then turned back to the other two.

"My father taught me to read some English, and the words painted on the metal can says the contents were made in your country," Pig Killer's son said with anger.

"And stolen by our enemies to kill our brothers and make us look guilty," the American man countered.

Stud Bull looked mollified. With sadness in his eyes, he asked, "Why would such a terrible thing be used on our people?"

"I want to see where the villagers died so I can find out," Hogan replied.

"But not until you have eaten and made the sounds of satisfaction."

The words came from Pig Killer, who handed Black Jack a metal plate on which was heaped a huge mound of venison and boiled greens.

The American was about to ask for a fork when he saw the other three greedily grabbing chunks of the meat and wild vegetables and shoving them in their mouths.

Hogan followed suit, and when they had eaten their fill, they picked themselves up and proceeded to the village.

There was a young woman waiting at the edge of the village as the jeep with Hogan and the three Lahu men pulled to a stop next to her.

Black haired with perfect features, she waved to them as she stood tall and proud in the rain, wearing only the black silk sarong.

To Hogan she was the most beautiful female he had seen since he had discovered Astrah. The smile she gave him, filled with perfect white teeth, was dazzling.

Stud Bull leaned across the front seat and elbowed the American with a grin. "You like? Her name is Ping."

Black Jack wasn't sure how to respond. "Ping is very pretty," he replied hastily.

The girl said something to Stud Bull in the clicking Lahu dialect, and he winked at Hogan.

"She thinks you are very pretty, too." The grin he wore now covered his entire face. "You want her?"

A sense of guilt washed over the American as he thought of the Kalabrian girl with wild-strawberry-colored hair.

"Not this second," he gulped diplomatically.

"Maybe later," the hill man concluded.

"Yes, maybe later," Black Jack agreed, grateful he had found the strength to reject the desirable offer.

Then he thought of something. "What is she doing here?"

Stud Bull turned to Ping and asked her Hogan's question in the Lahu dialect.

After she replied, the wiry hill man grunted, then faced Hogan. "She came to leave offerings around the edge of the village so that the evil spirits who did this terrible thing would stay here and not attack her village."

Black Jack looked at the girl quickly and saw she was carrying a large woven rattan tray filled with a large mound of meats, fruits and vegetables. Knowing that a truly full meal was a rare occasion among the Lahu, Hogan realized that the villagers who had sent her were so afraid of the demons they blamed for the death of the village's inhabitants that they were surrendering their supply of food to appease them.

"Tell her that evil spirits didn't do this to the villagers. Men did. Evil men."

The Lahu hunter shook his head. "She would not believe even me if I repeated your words. Until the men—if men did this thing—are brought before the Lahu for punishment, she and the others will believe that evil spirits are responsible.''

Hogan suspected that Stud Bull and the other two hunters were also among those who believed demons had murdered their kin.

''Then I shall have to find them and bring their bodies to show you,'' he said.

''I will go with you,'' Pig Killer announced with pride.

The other two men glanced at each other and quickly volunteered to join the hunt.

Pig Killer asked the obvious question, ''Where do we start?''

''Right here. I want to see the bodies—''

Stud Bull interrupted him. ''They were buried several moonlights ago. Are you asking us to dig them up?''

Black Jack remembered how filled with superstition the lives of the Lahu were. ''No,'' he decided, ''I will wander through the village to search for clues.''

He retrieved his CAR-15 from the jeep and checked to make sure there was a round in the chamber. Then loosened the automatic pistol and long knife that hung from the belt around his waist and grabbed the musette bag sitting on the floor.

Slipping the canvas strap of the bag around his neck, Hogan turned and waited while the three tribesmen quickly held a conference among themselves.

''We will wait for you here,'' Stud Bull announced, trying to hide his fear of the ghosts that inhabited the village. ''So we can capture any strangers who try to pass us.''

Black Jack Hogan suppressed a grin and nodded gravely. ''I will not be long.''

As Hogan turned to leave, Ping abruptly walked toward him, then stooped at the side of the man called Pig Killer and called out a phrase in the local dialect.

"What is she saying?" Hogan asked.

The Lahu hunter looked embarrassed. "She said to tell you she is not afraid of evil spirits. She will lead you to the grave we dug."

Boldly Ping moved to Black Jack's side. She pointed to a tiny cross attached to the chain around her neck. Hogan understood. She was trying to tell him she was a Christian and not afraid of the dead.

She smiled at him and took his hand. Then she led him into the deserted village.

To Black Jack, it felt as though he were entering one of the burial grounds of his native Southwest. He could feel the presence of the recent dead.

"Whey Mi," Ping said, waving her hand at the gathering of huts with thatched roofs.

Hogan looked puzzled.

"Whey Mi," she repeated, pointing to the rain-soaked dirt of the open area between the flimsy structures.

Finally he smiled with understanding. She was telling him that the name of this village was Whey Mi.

She pointed to a large soft mudlike mound of dirt just past the huts. Rotting fruits and vegetables were strewn across it.

The girl walked to it and gently tossed the food on her rattan tray on top of the mound, then rejoined Hogan. With gestures she indicated that under the mound were the bodies of the villagers and their animals. Black Jack remembered that the Lahu treated their farm animals like members of the family.

He nodded and started walking toward the burial site, but she grabbed his wrist. He stopped and looked at her.

She pointed to one of the huts and tried to pull him there.

Hogan wasn't sure what she had in mind and made a quick decision not to find out.

But she had already put her arms around his neck and pressed her body against his.

Before he could gently push her away, a series of explosions ruptured the stillness.

Ping shivered as a pair of slugs tore through her face and neck. Her almost-perfect features were suddenly replaced by a twisted mask of blood and torn tissue.

Without a sound she slid to the ground. Hogan could do nothing more, seeing that she was beyond help, and he threw himself to the ground and squirmed around to seek the source of the bullets.

All he could see was the thick forest in every direction.

Gripping his mini-Uzi, he elbow-crawled along the ground toward an outcropping of rocks behind which he could hide.

The hidden gunman opened fire again. Black Jack could identify the weapon now. A .50-caliber machine gun. Probably a Browning retrieved after the war.

The lead slugs tore a pattern of holes in the dark dirt as the American rolled out of their path.

Getting to his knees, he lunged for the safety of the rocks, barely reaching them before a third wave of gunfire chewed the ground around him.

Hogan was just wondering where the Lahu hunters were when he heard a second wave of rapid fire followed by screams of pain.

More than one armed attacker was hidden in the jungle. The second had succeeded in killing or injuring the tribesmen.

The shots had come from a low rise two hundred yards east of the village, and Hogan knew the 9 mm ammunition in his mini-Uzi wouldn't travel that far.

There were the Lahu's M-16s, but his chances of making it to the edge of the village were almost nil.

He nearly jumped when a deep voice beside him asked a question.

"Have you none of the thunder rocks?"

Startled at the unexpected company, Hogan swiveled around and saw Brom, looking larger than life with his vivid hair and beard. The American's eyes fell on the AK-47 the Kalabrian carried on his shoulder.

"No. I didn't think I needed them," he replied, then pointed to the automatic rifle. "Does that thing still have ammunition in it?"

"Of course," Brom replied. "I do not waste poison pellets."

Hogan restrained himself from asking since when, and gestured for the Kalabrian to hand him the weapon.

"Use this," he said, handing the mini-Uzi to Brom.

The warrior stared disdainfully at the small weapon. "It is a toy for a child," he grumbled.

"Only a child who wants to kill somebody," Black Jack replied, then sat with his back against the rock, ignored the drenching monsoon rains and tried to come up with a plan.

Brom joined him, wiping the rain from his face. "Is there ever a time when your world is pleasant?"

Hogan didn't bother answering. His mind was racing through a series of possible scenarios. Finally he put together one that might have a chance of succeeding.

"You keep firing in the direction the shots came from, while I sneak around and try to come behind the gunmen."

Brom was about to protest, but Hogan stopped him by starting to crawl out from behind the rocks.

Glaring at the American, Brom turned and rested the Uzi on a rock, then began to fire at the dense foliage in the distance.

Another wave of .50-caliber slugs splattered into the rocks in response.

Black Jack raced for the jungle and dived into it just as a burst from a hidden automatic weapon splintered a tree above him.

Elbowing his way along the soggy ground, Hogan froze as he saw a long scaly form slither past him.

It was a mountain viper, searching for food despite the rain. Hogan got an idea. Carefully he grabbed the deadly serpent behind its head and half stood. The angry snake was trying to free itself, hissing and spitting as it twisted its powerful body. But Black Jack hung on, turned in the general direction of the gunfire and threw the snake with the overhand swing of a major-league pitcher.

Terrified curses in Vietnamese traveled through the vine-thick forest as the snake landed.

He had found where the gunmen were hiding.

Rapidly weaving his way between the thick clusters of bamboo, Hogan soon spotted the hidden machine gun, sitting on the edge of the low rise, aimed at the dead village.

Two black-clad soldiers were there. One had grabbed the viper and was trying to chop its head off with a machetelike jungle knife.

Hogan stopped his struggles with a short burst from the AK-47 in his hands. All three tumblers crashed their way into the preoccupied man's chest and neck.

Thick crimson fluid spurted from ruptured vessels as the shattered jungle fighter dropped the serpent. The triangular-headed snake pulled back, then darted forward and sank its fangs into the fallen Asian's face.

A second man stared in horror at the reptile, then turned and saw the American. Quickly he twisted the barrel of the tripod-mounted machine gun around and jammed his finger into the trigger housing.

Hogan dived out of the path of the .50-caliber death-seekers and skidded on the soggy ground. Mud splattered into his face and eyes, blinding him.

Pushing his AK-47 in the direction of the machine-gun clatter, Black Jack squeezed his trigger and moved his automatic weapon in a wide arc as he emptied his clip.

A soft grunt told him he had hit his mark. Wiping the mud from his eyes, he rolled into the nearby broom grass and jerked his 9 mm Beretta from its holster.

Then he took a cautious look at the machine-gun placement.

A black figure was draped across the barrel of the weapon.

There was the sound of footsteps coming from behind. Hogan swirled and raised his automatic pistol, ready to pull the trigger. But it was Brom who emerged from the foliage, carrying a pair of heads by their hair.

"These two were hiding near the entrance to the village," he said, throwing the severed heads into the woods. Then he shoved the huge broadsword in his hand back into a shoulder scabbard.

Hogan looked for the weapon he had handed the Kalabrian.

"What happened to the gun?"

"I emptied its poison pellets on a third man, then it refused to continue killing, so I threw it away."

Black Jack pulled himself to his feet. He could feel the wrenched muscles in his body throbbing as he brushed the mud from his work shirt and jeans.

He didn't want to explain just then the workings of a gun to his Kalabrian brother-in-arms. Instead, he pointed through the trees to the ghost village below. "Like the village Mondlock had us visit, the people who lived here died of poison gas."

"Poison gas?"

"There are places in our world where vapor that can kill rises from deep cracks in the ground. But no one lives near them."

"Men made this poison gas? What kind of twisted mind would create such hideous a weapon?"

It would be too difficult to explain to Brom the kind of politics that made maintaining inventories of poison gas and bacteriological weapons essential. Especially since Hogan didn't understand them, either.

"It's not who made them, but who is using them that matters."

"But this poison gas has been used in your world and in mine. How could that happen?"

A stunned expression spread across Brom's face as he came up with the only explanation. "The alien creature," he said, his voice hollow.

Hogan looked grim. "Who else?"

"Then Mondlock is right. There is no hope for our worlds."

"Let's wait until after we're dead to decide that," Hogan put in quickly. "Meantime, I've got to find out where he got the poison gas and how to get it back before more is released."

"I will stay and assist you."

"No. You've got a ceremony to get ready for, and first I have to find some answers. Just keep your troops alert to any more attacks with poison gas."

The two men grasped each other's forearm.

"Find a way to stop him, Hogan."

"You do the same."

And God help our worlds if we don't, Hogan told himself as he watched Brom move inside the shimmering cloud that had just appeared.

14

"Get me that doctor at SOG," Hiram Wilson shouted to his secretary as he read the report from the laboratory at Walter Reed Hospital for the fifth time.

He started to pick up the unlit Cuban cigar that sat in his ashtray and light it. Before he could, Mrs. Bolivar poked her head into his office.

"Dr. Weinfeild is on three," she said calmly.

Wilson snatched the phone from the receiver and yelled into it. "Did you read the report I faxed you?"

"Yes. What about it?"

"How did traces of VX gas get in the blood?"

"Probably it was inhaled. That's the way poison gas is supposed to work," the voice replied patiently.

Wilson didn't answer. He was too busy wondering where Hogan had gotten the blood specimen. It could have been an overlooked canister of VX left over from Vietnam that had been found and accidentally released. He vocalized his thoughts to the Special Operations Group official on the phone.

"It's possible. VX missiles occasionally still turn up from as far back as World War II when the Germans were stockpiling them."

Wilson became aware of his secretary standing in the doorway again. He looked up at her and clamped a hand on the telephone mouthpiece.

"What is it?"

"Admiral Demming is on line two. He says it's urgent." She paused. "And the President's secretary called. He wants you in his office immediately."

Wilson terminated the conversation with the SOG scientist and picked up line two.

"Something wrong, Admiral?"

"I'm not sure. We flew a crew of specialists to the area where we last heard from the *Murman* to test the waters. They found no traces of VX or GB gas pollution. As an added precaution, we sent a team of divers from Hawaii to search for the wreckage, but they came up empty-handed."

Wilson ended the call abruptly and leaned back in his large leather chair. Waving his still-unlit cigar in the air like a baton, he asked himself the same question he had asked since the small package from Hogan had arrived: where did his field agent get the sample?

He buzzed for his secretary again. When she stepped into his office, he asked, "Did Hogan say where he was going when he called the other day?"

"All I know is that he called from Bangkok and was heading north."

Wilson dropped the pose of the soft-spoken Southerner as he snapped an order to Mrs. Bolivar. "Get a priority-one out to all stations. I need to talk to Black Jack now. Find him, wherever he is!"

She left the office to place the calls, and Hiram Wilson resumed staring at the report.

Perhaps the culprit was a long-forgotten gas canister or bomb left behind in an Indo-Chinese paddy after the Americans pulled out. Live missiles still turned up there— sometimes with tragic consequences. And, as he remembered, the military hadn't been too selective back then about where they dropped their deadly eggs.

The only one who might know was Black Jack Hogan, and he had vanished.

Usually Wilson was tolerant about Hogan's frequent disappearances. Despite his insistence on doing things his own way, Black Jack always completed his assigned missions.

This time was different. There had been no mission. At least not yet.

He picked up the cigar that sat in his ashtray and rolled it between his fingers as he wondered what was going on.

The same question kept coming back to haunt him. Where had Hogan gotten the sample? Then another thought forced its way to the forefront of his mind. What if the hundred thousand poison gas shells and canisters had not been lost at sea? For a moment he refused to accept that possibility, then the carefully developed pragmatism acquired over many years of service with the CIA took charge, and another question entered his mind.

If the material hadn't been lost at sea, in whose possession was it? And for what reason?

The range of possibilities frightened him, and he ran his fingers through his hair. At last he stood up and straightened his tie. He had been summoned to the President's office, and he knew what the outcome would be. Black Jack Hogan, who already seemed peripherally involved, would be charged with another mission.

As soon as Hiram Wilson made his way back from the White House, Mrs. Bolivar accosted him excitedly.

"Black Jack is calling from the American Embassy in Bangkok."

Hiram Wilson grabbed the phone and pressed down on the line with the flashing light, then barked, "Are you on a secured line?"

"Yes."

"Tell me where you got that blood sample."

There was silence on the other end for a second, then Hogan asked, "Why?"

"Because it was contaminated with—"

Wilson caught himself. Even on a secured line he had to be cautious. One hint of the missing cargo, and there would be panic around the world and riots against the Americans who had manufactured the gas.

"We must meet and talk in person."

He weighed various locations, then selected one he hadn't used in many years.

"Take a flight to Singapore and meet me at the Raffles Hotel."

"When?"

"Right now!" The words cracked like a whip.

"I need clothes and equipment."

"I'll bring everything you need. Give me a list."

Grabbing a pad and pen, he started writing as his agent talked. Finally the list was complete.

"There's something else I want to ask," he said while he pushed the buzzer for his secretary.

The door opened and Mrs. Bolivar appeared.

"Hold on," he snapped into the phone. Then he turned to Mrs. Bolivar. "Call Weinfield at Special Operations Group and read this to him."

He scribbled some words on his pad, then tore off the page and handed it to her.

"Then contact General Wollaston at Fort Meade and read him the top half of this list," he continued, handing her the page with the items Hogan had requested. "You buy the rest of them. I want everything here in three hours, before I leave for Andrews Air Force Base to get the military jet you're going to line up for me."

"To fly where?"

"Singapore. Call the State Department and make the arrangements. If anybody gives you a hard time, tell them to call the President."

Unruffled at the demands, Mrs. Bolivar left the office and closed the door behind herself.

Wilson focused his attention on the telephone again. "Now, tell me where you got the blood sample," he demanded. But Hogan had already hung up.

15

"I've gotten several calls from reporters asking about rumors that the aborigines are staging a protest against Gaia," Marco reported.

Kalidonian looked at him impassively. "Get rid of the bodies before any nosy newsmen show up," he ordered.

"How?"

"Take a crew with you and bury them."

"The wild dogs will dig them up." Marco hesitated, then continued. "Karla had a suggestion."

"What did she propose?"

"That we bring the bodies inside. Then when reporters show up, she could meet them outside and, as a fellow reporter, convince them there was no truth to the rumors."

Kalidonian weighed Marco's words, then turned to Dr. Nis, who stood with his back against a wall, listening quietly.

"Do you have any suggestions?"

Nis weighed his options, then nodded. "I'll take care of them," he promised.

Marco wasn't satisfied.

"How?"

"How is irrelevant. What matters is that by tomorrow their bodies will not be outside the biosphere."

Marco decided not to pursue his questioning. There was something about Dr. Nis that had begun to make him feel uneasy. It was nothing specific, except that he seemed to vanish frequently without explaining where he had been.

Marco wanted nothing to interfere with the plans Nis and he had made. The best of the activist groups had been brought here to join him in taking charge of what would remain of the world after the gas shells had been released.

Groups from Armenia, El Salvador, the Middle East, then the IRA, the Italian Red Brigade, even the Liberation Tigers of Tamil Eelam from Sri Lanka and the Sikh Babbar Khalsa had come here to join with the other movements and participate in the new civilization that was about to be started under his leadership.

Already teams of mercenaries were busy placing the pirated shells where they could create the most terror. The population of major cities like New York, Washington, D.C., Chicago, Los Angeles, London, Paris, Rome, Tokyo, New Delhi, Tel Aviv, Buenos Aires, Moscow and a two dozen more would soon face the grim finality of death.

He touched his pocket and felt the thick sheaf of pages in his pocket. This was the list he had worked out with representatives of the various movements of where the shells would be hidden in each of the target cities.

At his command, to be broadcast twenty-seven days from now, members of the various movements, protected by contamination suits and gas masks, were scheduled to release the poison gas. Then they were to make their way to Gaia.

Then he realized he had not yet selected a code word for the command. He would have to decide and have the word passed along....

Something warned him, and when he looked at Kalidonian, he realized the man had been talking to him.

"You were daydreaming," Kalidonian gently chastised him.

Marco nodded. "I was thinking of something I needed to take care of."

"I see. Now, we don't need to impose on Karla," Kalidonian said happily as Nis turned and strolled out of the office.

AS HE WALKED along the corridor, Nis decided that the bodies of the aborigines would be discovered in some remote part of Kalabria. Their presence would serve to bring the creature who called himself Brom to view them, and then Peytok and his hirelings could get rid of him.

Suddenly Nis felt an overwhelming desire to sit down and rest. His body was rapidly losing its store of energy. He would have to accelerate the timetable so that he could complete his search before the power was gone.

He entered his room and locked the door behind him. As he lay down on the narrow bed, he knew a decision had been made.

The form that was Nis began to slowly fade until it was gone.

The small dark shadow that hovered in a corner of the room shut down its functions. Energy had to be conserved until more could be found.

The last of the Guardians had to survive.

KARLA HAD WAITED until everyone but a handful of well-armed guards had retired to their rooms. One of them stopped her as she strolled around the parklike square that sat in the center of the biosphere.

"Something wrong, Miss Hamilton?"

"No. I think I'm just too excited thinking about what's going to happen soon and I can't sleep."

The guard grinned. "I know what you mean. It's like helping to give birth to a new world."

While you destroy the old one, she thought. But she replied, "Exactly. I was hoping the fresh air—" she smiled

"—the filtered, fresh air," she said, correcting herself, "would help me relax."

The guard was about to answer when a small buzzer went off on the pager he carried on his belt.

"It's time to check another sector," he said, shutting off the pager. "Enjoy your stroll."

Karla waited until he vanished, then walked to the shell that separated the biosphere from the outside world and pressed a button.

The panel slid aside and revealed a small port window.

Even in the darkness she could make out the bodies. She needed pictures to expose what Kalidonian and his team were doing. She had been smart enough to bring some infrared film with her.

Nausea swept over her as she photographed the senseless slaughter of the innocent men with her tiny camera.

It was just like the village in Thailand.

Forcing the tears of terror down, she hurried back to her room.

Kalidonian had promised to use the poison gas he claimed to possess only if the governments of the world didn't step down and allow his representatives to take over.

And the day of the announcement was three weeks away.

Now she understood Marco's map and list. They were the cities targeted to be destroyed and the list was the location of the containers of deadly gas.

She had to pass the information on to somebody who could stop Kalidonian and his henchmen.

She searched her mind, then remembered a special agent for the United States government she had attempted to interview after he supposedly had stopped a Middle Eastern dictator from poisoning the water supplies of neighboring countries prior to invading them.

His name wouldn't come to her, and she randomly went through different surnames to relax her mind. At last the name popped up from her subconscious.

Hogan. John Hogan.

She had gone to the Buddhist temple in Cambodia where he was reputed to live between missions to get an exclusive interview with him. But he refused to talk to her, even after she contacted a top White House aide named Hiram Wilson, who was supposedly his official contact.

If she could get her films to the American Embassy in Australia, she was sure they could find a way to deliver them to John Hogan.

The trouble was, she knew Kalidonian wouldn't let her out of his sight until he had made his public declaration. At least not alive.

16

When Hogan landed in Singapore, he knew he was facing an unpleasant ordeal. When he was disembarking, there had been an attempt on his life, but unfortunately one of the attendants had taken the poison dart that had been meant for him. Not only that, but Brom had also appeared, and he had taken care of one of the assailants in his usual manner. The man's arm had been severed by Brom's sword, and he had bled to death. There was another accomplice, a female, and Hogan had been forced to dispatch her with a blow to the heart that he had learned from Mok Seng.

The passengers had been stunned, naturally, and some of them babbled incoherently about a giant red-bearded man who just disappeared into thin air, a rider of the apocalypse. The police had arrived on the scene quickly, and now there would be no end to their questioning.

He was whisked away from Changi Airport to police headquarters.

The city outside the car's windows seemed to be drowning in the monsoon rains, and it was likely to keep up for the next five weeks. Looking at the streaming city, Hogan resigned himself to the upcoming tedium of the police procedure.

The interrogation lasted for hours.

Finally the Singapore police seemed prepared to accept Hogan's claim that he was as puzzled by the attack in the airplane cabin as were the other passengers, except for Chang, the chief interrogator, who still wasn't satisfied the American had told him the truth.

As a captain in the Singapore security police, he had a thick file on an American agent named John Hogan and on the two assailants, both North Koreans, who had been slaughtered with a bladed weapon. They were former secret police agents who had turned free-lance terrorists.

Some of the reports garnered from the secret police of other countries claimed that the American was a professional executioner for his government. Others reported that Hogan was an agent intent on destroying major drug suppliers. Several believed that his prime function was preventing dictators from invading their neighbors. One or two voiced different opinions.

The few things they agreed upon was his Cambodian residence between assignments, and that he was good at his job.

Possibly the best.

Chang had read the file before coming into the interrogation room. Despite his persistence and veiled threats, the American continued to claim he had only been an innocent passenger of the flight from Bangkok.

The security captain took a different tack.

"What about the severed body parts of the elderly man?"

"Things like that make me sick," Black Jack replied blandly.

Chang was about to resort to a more physical form of interrogation when he was interrupted by the opening of the door to the room.

As he looked up, two men entered.

He recognized one of them immediately: a dignified, well-dressed man with neatly trimmed steel gray hair.

Lee Wan was a special aide to the prime minister. Some said he dealt with those aspects of Singapore's relations with other countries that couldn't be handled through normal diplomatic channels.

The other was a young, haughty-looking American dressed in the dark gray pin-striped suit uniform of embassy officials.

"Mr. Leland, from the American Embassy, and I have come for this man," Lee Wan announced in a thin, prissy voice.

There was no point in protesting. Not if Chang wanted to continue his career with the security police.

Without saying a word, he got up from his chair and left the room.

The Singapore prime minister's aide lifted the still-damp raincoat from the back of the door and handed it to Hogan.

"Mr. Leland will take you to your appointment," he said, then withdrew from the room.

As HOGAN APPROACHED the suite, he could smell the sweet aroma of tobacco.

Wilson was so fond of Cuban cigars that he insisted that the merchant in London who shipped him a fresh box each week remove the cigar bands and labels identifying the country of origin.

Hogan was glad Thomas Leland hadn't accompanied him to Wilson's suite.

To ride in the Embassy limousine had been boring. Leland had ordered the driver to take them on a brief tour of the city.

Leland had obviously done his homework on Singapore, and persisted in pounding his library-acquired education at Hogan's ears.

"Three quarters of the citizens of Singapore are of Chinese descent. The rest are Malays, Tamils, Sikhs, Bengalis, Caucasians and Eurasians," Leland had lectured. "Singapore is a country with only one city—Singapore." He'd laughed at his unfunny joke, then continued. "It is called the 'cash register of Asia' because so many of the banks in East Asia are headquartered here. You can buy any kind of food you want here, or clothing or jewelry. Actually anything else." Leland had pointed out of his window at a narrow street filled with bar signs. The corner sign read Burgis Street.

Leland had inspected Hogan's jeans, work shirt and dusty black cowboy boots. "Including any kind of companion you want to spend the night with."

When the limousine had pulled up in front of the venerable Raffles Hotel, a historical landmark in Singapore, he looked at Hogan hopefully. "Would you like me to come up?"

"No," Black Jack had replied.

"If you have time this evening," Leland had continued, unwilling to surrender his thin grip on a near-celebrity among American Embassy officials, "I could introduce you to some ladies I know you'd really enjoy."

"Let's see what my boss has in mind first."

"I'll wait at my desk for your call," Leland had said by way of a goodbye.

I hope you have a change of clothes at the office, Hogan had thought as he waited for the uniformed doorman to open the limousine door.

As Hogan came up before the suite, he breathed a sigh of relief to be free of Leland. He knocked, expecting to be greeted by an impeccably dressed man. The White House aide played the role of the Southern gentleman flawlessly when he chose, right down to speaking in a low, well-modulated voice.

The door opened, and what Black Jack saw was an angry man whose clothes looked as if he'd slept in them.

Hogan looked surprised. "What happened to you?"

"I've been up all night, thanks to you," the disheveled man growled.

"Me?" Until the CIA man at the Bangkok Embassy greeted him at Don Muang Airport, he hadn't known Wilson was trying to find him.

Wilson pulled him into the suite and slammed the door.

"Get out of that coat," he ordered.

Hogan slipped it off and let it fall to the carpeted floor.

Wilson sighed. "Before we talk about anything else, what happened on the plane?"

Black Jack had learned to be precise with the Intelligence aide.

"Three people died. An Oriental couple and an airplane employee. One of them, the Oriental woman, swallowed cyanide—or something like it—and committed suicide."

"How did the man's arm get cut off?"

Hogan forced his eyes to become expressionless.

"I haven't got a clue."

Wilson smiled sarcastically. "I'll bet you don't. This isn't the first time this kind of thing has happened around you." He dropped the sarcasm. "Come on, Black Jack, level with me."

"There are a lot of sick weirdos in this world, boss," Hogan replied, hoping he had captured just the right amount of shock and disgust in his voice.

Hiram Wilson studied his face for a minute—as if he thought he could find some answers in it—then gave up and sat down in a chair near an antique desk.

"These are the results we ran on the blood sample you sent," he snapped. "Do you know what they say?"

"Yes. There were traces of poison gas in the sample."

The man from Washington exploded with a barrage of questions. "Where did the sample come from? What do you know about poison gas? Where have you—"

Hogan interrupted him. "You are the one who has to tell me more first."

Wilson took deep breaths to help calm down. He dropped the laboratory report and picked up another sheaf of papers.

"What's going on is this," he said, handing them to his agent.

Black Jack started to scan them, then moved to a chair and sat down while he continued reading. His eyes opened wider as he turned page after page.

"There was enough VX and GB gas in the hold of that cargo ship to wipe out the Earth's population."

"Enough to wipe it out two or three times," Wilson replied.

"Why would anyone want to steal it?"

Then he remembered the village in Thailand and the one in Brom's land. There was only one who could use the poison in both worlds. It had to be Nis.

To share his knowledge with the pragmatic man from Washington would only lead to his being locked up in a military mental ward for observation. He left his own question unanswered.

"You find out," Wilson snapped, picking up an unlit cigar from his ashtray and biting down on it. "And get those shells and canisters back."

"Great," Hogan muttered. "Got any leads?"

"I haven't got a clue. But here's some information that may help." He picked up a thick stack of photographs. "One hell of a lot of terrorist leaders have suddenly vanished from their usual haunts. Which may or may not have anything to do with the gas."

"Anybody know where they were heading?"

"Copies of those photographs were passed around, and we came up with some immigration officials in Darwin,

Australia, who swear some of them were spotted entering the country under another name."

Black Jack gazed out of a window at the colorful parade of people strolling on the street below.

Talking to himself, he asked, "What the hell is in Australia that would interest a terrorist?"

Wilson perused a typewritten page and answered the question. "Maybe they decided to become tourists. There are crocodiles, kangaroos, aborigines, a lot of sacred places the aborigines worship. An experimental biosphere has been constructed by a rich industrialist. It's supposed to help find ways to solve the ecology problems of the world. Probably it's an industrialist who's guilty about all the pollution and acid rain he's put in the atmosphere. Then there are sheep and cattle, a lot of beer and ale—and uranium mines."

"I'll put my money on the uranium."

"We alerted the Australian government. They've assigned their best forces to baby-sit the mines. We're flying down a planeload of contamination gear and the latest antidotes."

He reached under a table and pulled out a quilted carry-on bag. "Which reminds me. There are a dozen vials of injectable antidote and tubes of ointment in here if you accidentally get exposed to the gas. And you'll find two contamination outfits packed with the equipment you requested waiting for you at Changi Airport."

Hogan sounded skeptical. "Does the stuff work?"

"The antidote? Naturally the less exposed you are the more effective it is. But of course it works."

At least in laboratory tests, Wilson admitted to himself silently.

Though he felt more affection for Hogan than he had ever felt for any other man, the mission came first.

Still, he hoped the antidote would work if it was needed. Hogan would be hard to replace.

It was time for his field agent to get started.

"There's a military helicopter waiting to fly you back to the temple. Your equipment's already aboard."

He hesitated, then continued. "One last thing. If the press gets wind of this, there'll be a lot of people around the world getting hysterical," he warned.

"If I don't get the shells and canisters back, it won't matter," Black Jack Hogan called back over his shoulder, then the door banged shut behind him.

THE U.S. ARMY'S Hughes OH-6A Cayuse helicopter hovered over the sodden clearing near the Buddhist temple.

Hogan looked down at the vast ruins where ancient kings once lived, and the temple that was the only structure there that housed the living.

He leaned over and tapped the pilot on the shoulder.

"Set her down on the field. The monks will help me carry the cases and duffel bags inside," he shouted over the loud roar of the powerful rotors.

The pilot, Captain Mort Caldwell, gave Black Jack a thumbs-up, then gestured to his copilot, Lieutenant Phil Simon, to commence the landing sequence.

Slowly the clumsy-looking aircraft touched the ground with the gentleness of a feather.

The American agent scampered out of the helicopter. He could feel the rain race through his hair and down his neck into his shirt.

It didn't matter. He was home.

The two pilots looked at the rain and hesitated, then shouted, "What the hell."

They jumped out of their helicopter to stretch their legs.

They'd waited for hours at Don Muang Airport for the small Army jet to arrive from Singapore. Then, under orders from the colonel in charge of transportation, they had helped load the cargo into their utility helicopter without a break for lunch.

The tall man had climbed into one of the seats behind them.

Most of the passengers they transported to various locations in Indochina chattered endlessly about where they had been, where they were going or what their jobs were.

But not this passenger. He seemed almost reluctant to talk, even when they probed with questions.

They wondered what someone who looked as though he was at home in combat was doing traveling to a Buddhist temple.

Black Jack felt a slight letdown. Usually a half dozen would rush out to stare at the helicopter, then offer to help him carry his boxes inside.

This time nobody had appeared.

For a moment Hogan considered whether they were in meditation.

But no, he would have heard the bell calling them. Even from the sky.

Perhaps there was some special holiday. He ran down a list in his mind of the ones he knew. There was none around this time of the year.

Something was wrong. He could sense it, but he wasn't sure what.

He returned to the airship.

"Got a spare weapon?"

Captain Caldwell was surprised at the request.

"Any problems?"

Hogan shook his head. "I'm not sure."

The pilot turned to Lieutenant Simon. "Dig up one of them Uzis we bartered Jack Daniel's for," he ordered.

The junior officer climbed to the rear of the helicopter and knelt down. Finally he got to his feet and handed Hogan an Uzi.

He was in luck. The clip was full, and he jacked a round into the chamber.

"Can you hang around for a few minutes? I'll be back."

The captain nodded.

HOGAN MOVED SLOWLY through the tall grass, carefully flattening a path to the small temple. He moved a few feet, then stopped and listened.

There were no sounds, except for the incessant chatter of birds and insects.

The hairs on his neck began to grow stiff as he came closer to the stone structure that housed thirty-five monks.

Where were they? he wondered. He settled for one of them showing up and telling him where the others had gone.

He looked ahead and stopped in his tracks.

He had found one of the monks.

He was dead.

Checking the area with his eyes, Hogan scanned every inch of ground around him. His forehead was becoming moist.

If there were any in hiding, he couldn't spot them.

Cautiously he moved to the body and knelt beside it.

Hogan didn't recognize him.

Probably one of the young men sent to serve three months as a monk by his family, he decided.

This one would never serve again, in any capacity.

The American agent studied the dead man's face carefully. There was nothing to indicate what had killed him.

He got down on his knees and leaned close to the body. He sniffed, checking for the aroma of almonds—the odor of cyanide.

Nothing.

He got to his feet. He'd come back and do something about the body later.

He continued to approach the temple stealthily.

There were two more bodies on the ground. Both had been monks. Now they were lifeless sacks of flesh and bones.

Next he saw a shadow leaning against a wall of the temple. He moved quickly to it, and found a fourth body.

He was bewildered, not knowing what could have happened.

Then he remembered the two villages, and was catapulted into a forward rush.

"Mok Seng," he shouted, racing into the temple.

He found still bodies everywhere. Even in the great meditation hall.

Young monks and older ones. The body of a small boy who must have been a visitor.

Hogan searched the faces in dread of finding the one he was seeking.

Room after room he searched and found more bodies, but not that of the abbot.

Either Mok Seng's body was hidden, or he wasn't dead.

Hogan looked at the giant bronze statue of the potbellied figure that was supposed to be Buddha.

"If you really have any power, just make sure that bad-tempered, pint-sized monk who likes to push me around is still alive," he growled angrily, coming as close to a prayer as he could.

Emotionally exhausted, Black Jack leaned against one of the walls and felt a dampness on his face.

He never cried for anyone or anything until now.

But he lived with these men and meditated with them.

They were harmless men seeking some spiritual explanation for their existence—and found only death, probably because he'd been among them.

He heard voices behind him and raised the Uzi to his shoulder.

Turning to face them, he forced his finger against the trigger, then took it away when he saw the pilots, armed with Uzis, walking into the meditation hall. Both of them looked horror-struck.

The pilot found his voice first. "Who would want to kill a bunch of harmless Buddhist priests?"

Hogan shook his head and turned his eyes from them.

There was no point panicking them until he was sure.

The younger pilot found it difficult to express his feelings. "This stinks, man," he finally managed to say. "This really stinks."

"Yes," Black Jack replied in a hollow voice.

They shuffled around aimlessly for a while. Then the two pilots helped Hogan gather the bodies and line them up in the meditation hall.

"We could help you dig a mass grave," Caldwell offered.

"I don't know what kind of rites they should have before they're buried. But thanks," Hogan said, wearily. "I'll contact somebody at the Buddhist temple in Battambang and ask what I should do."

Together the three returned to the helicopter for the equipment.

The two large metal cases and two duffel bags were deposited into Hogan's room.

Black Jack walked them to the front of the temple, where he shook hands with them.

"Thanks for your help."

"I hope you never have to reciprocate," Captain Caldwell replied. "Sure you don't want to fly back to Bangkok?"

Hogan shook his head, then turned and walked slowly back into the temple. In his sense of desolation, he thought of Brom, and in his mind's eye saw the warrior riding in bright sunlight, then a dark gloom swallowed him.

BROM AND HIS TROOPS had left Tella far behind. Strange reports of a pile of dark-skinned painted bodies—such as never had been seen in the land—were bringing them closer to the village of Krendok every minute.

The closer they got, the more Brom felt the heavy chill of evil settle on his shoulders.

There was an unease in the air. He could tell his men felt it from their gloomy expressions. Even the horses moved forward reluctantly.

Captain Zhuzak rode up to him.

"Something here feels odd, Lord Brom," the black-bearded commander muttered.

Privately Brom agreed with him. But the existence of the strange bodies needed to be investigated, and when he'd talked to Mondlock, he had committed to carrying out that task.

His face assumed a scowl. This was no time to admit fear.

"Are we warriors—or frightened women?"

Zhuzak was startled by the question. With a hurt expression, he turned away and rode back to his men without answering.

Brom repeated the question loudly. "Are we warriors or frightened women?"

This time the men raised their eyes and looked at him. He stared at them defiantly. "Answer me," he yelled.

"Warriors!" Zhuzak shouted back without enthusiasm.

One by one the mounted troops joined in the response. Their voices grew louder as they repeated the word.

"Warriors. Warriors. Warriors."

Brom forced a smile on his face.

"Good. Then let's not hear of evil and magic haunting this place, and ride instead with determination to defend Kalabria from its enemies."

Then he gave the signal, and slowly led his troops along the unpaved road that led to Krendok.

BLACK JACK had opened a large case and taken out one of the pair of Colt M-16A1 automatic rifles with M-203 grenade launchers and a handful of 20-round clips for the powerful combination weapon.

Now he sat on the rain-drenched ground with the battle-ready weapon on his lap, staring at the large open grave with the bodies neatly lined up like toy figures.

Like the bodies he had seen in the Thai village and the hamlet in Kalabria, their faces and bodies were covered with sores and blisters from contact with the poison gas that had killed them.

He had seen much death in his life. He had seen friends and enemies die in a thousand gruesome ways. Torn to shreds by the machines and madness of war and hate. Villagers put to sleep forever by poison gas.

He himself had died, or thought he had, only to be told by the devil he wasn't welcome in hell.

Brom had told the same story about himself.

But as many times as he had been a witness to death, it still came as a new and painful reality.

He looked as if he still couldn't comprehend the horror he had discovered. The bodies were once men with whom he had shared food and meditation. Some of them he admired for their serenity or patience. Others had made him laugh with their foolish pranks. He had shared a joke with some of them or complained about his hard bed, the dampness of the temple and the unappetizing food.

Now he was the sole survivor except for Mok Seng, unless he, too, was also dead and his body yet undiscovered.

Hogan felt cheated. The only real home he had known as an adult had been invaded and sullied.

A shimmering cloud began to form across the open field, but Hogan was too filled with grief to raise his head to see it. Even when his instincts told him to look.

But the shock was beginning to wear off, and a deep anger began to replace it. At those who had murdered these men of peace.

Hogan made a silent vow to find those responsible and make them pay.

"You will do it," a soft voice behind him said quietly, as if whoever it was had read his mind.

Gripping the automatic rifle, Black Jack turned his head and saw Mok Seng's calm face.

A flash of joy lit Hogan's eyes, but it was replaced by one of sadness as he turned back to the large open grave.

"They were all dead when I got back," he said.

"And you feel you are to blame?"

"Yes. It was me they were after."

"Evil destroys everything that is good and pure."

"But they'd be alive if I hadn't been living here."

"Perhaps. But there would be another time and another evil that needed to destroy the temple and those who kept it alive."

"You're lucky you weren't here or you would be dead, too."

"Yes. It was Buddha's doing that my eyeglasses did not fit properly and I had to drive myself to Battambang."

Even filled with sorrow as he was, Black Jack winced at the thought of the monk driving a vehicle. He had witnessed too many near-accidents when he let Mok Seng get behind the wheel.

He had a dangerous habit of allowing his eyes to roam in every direction as he discovered new wonders. As many times as Hogan had tried, he couldn't convince Mok Seng that not keeping his eyes on the road could be fatal.

"I was going to bury them," Hogan apologized. "But I wasn't sure what kind of ritual they should have."

"I will have monks from other temples nearby come and help me send them on their journey. It is written in the proverbs that 'life is a dreaming walking and death is a going home.' My holy children are now bound for their eternal home."

"I can help."

"No. You have a journey to undertake to find those responsible and stop them from repeating their evil on others."

Hogan started to protest, but Mok Seng cut him off. "It is your destiny. Gather up the things you need and begin your travels."

The shimmering cloud hovered as long as it could, then finally became transparent and disappeared.

Black Jack knew the monk was right. He started to walk toward the temple to retrieve the gear Wilson had sent. Then he halted and faced Mok Seng again.

He fished for the right words for this farewell.

"I will be waiting here when you get back. So we can continue your lessons," Mok Seng said with a small smile.

17

Krendok lay in a hollow of fertile land, surrounded by buttes on the north and south. A hundred families inhabited the community and the rich land around it.

They were tillers of the soil and animal husbanders, raising enough food to feed themselves and ship to marketplaces where buyers from the cities came to find provisions to sell.

But none of them were in evidence this late afternoon. Most had fled as Peytok's troops charged through the countryside, raping, stealing and slaying as they went.

Only their dead stayed behind. Fifty bodies, mourned but still unburied. And near them were the dark skinned bodies who had mysteriously appeared there. More than two hundred of them.

At last Brom and his hundred warriors came upon the ruined village, armed and ready for combat.

Their shields were raised, swords drawn and grasped by the same hands that held the reins of their mounts. Scabbarded kralls had been loosened so they could be pulled from their ornate sheaths easily, and tucked into loops on their saddles were honed battle-axs and maces.

Three dozen of the Kalabrian force were expert with the short battle bow. Their gut-strung weapons were fitted with long wooden shafts tipped with barbed metal arrowheads.

Leading them into the hollow was the giant red-bearded warrior, brandishing the huge broadsword that made a howling sound as he cleaved the air with it.

"Show yourselves, cowards!" he shouted as a challenge.

His men took up the cry. "Cowards, come face your future," they yelled in unison.

Then the Nordian invader, Peytok, appeared on top of one of the buttes.

Seated on a horse and dressed in full armor, he yelled out his response.

"Here you all die, Kalabrians, along with your leader, Brom. Then Kalabria becomes a part of Nordia."

"Only if you win, man lover," Brom yelled back.

Peytok had a reputation for taking on male lovers.

"Your bride-to-be will wear black at your funeral, Kalabrian," Peytok shouted angrily.

"And I shall deliver your male organs in a gilded box to your bedmate," the red-beard promised loudly, then spurred his horse and led his men toward the butte.

Peytok vanished from view, but from every direction a host of soldiers appeared—more than five hundred of them.

Some were mounted though most were on foot, but all were armed with heavy weapons capable of snuffing out life with a single blow.

Wearing the horned helmets that symbolized their temporary allegiance to Peytok, they screamed their battle cries as they charged forward.

The Kalabrians let loose their arrows at the advancing enemy, and some of them fell back with startled cries. But quickly the ranks of the combatants closed, with the clashing of swords and the grunting of men who fought ferociously.

Horsemen fell or were pulled out of their saddles to continue fighting on foot, while those engaged in struggles on the ground stumbled about. Soon kralls came into play, flashing brightly in the sun.

Brom was charging in and out of the crowded battle-ground, slashing and jabbing at the horn-helmeted enemy, helping his men when he saw them cornered.

His long heavy sword was crimson edged, and when he paused for a moment, he saw Zhuzak in pitched battle.

Zhuzak was grinning fiercely as he leaned down from his saddle and dueled three soldiers at the same time. Then he jumped from his horse to challenge the trio on foot.

A clanging resounded in the air as he brought his sword into play, moving surprisingly fast for his weight.

"You move well for a fat man," one of the opponents taunted.

With a powerful downward motion, Zhuzak sliced through the man's wrist and glanced at the bleeding hand lying on the ground.

"Pick it up," he ordered as he held the other two at bay.

The stunned soldier reached down to retrieve the fallen appendage, and the Kalabrian flicked his heavy short sword and cut through the neck of the kneeling man.

The partially attached head lolled forward as the man's life ebbed away in a crimson flow.

Zhuzak bared his teeth at the other two facing him. "Anyone else want to take on a fat man?"

They hesitated, then raised their weapons to attack.

But the Kalabrian didn't wait for the swords to reach him. He rammed the tip of his blade at the chain-link armor protecting the midsection of one opponent, while he dodged the slashing blade of the other. The power of his muscled arms drove the blade into the mercenary's solar plexus. With a twist of his hand, the Kalabrian captain tore through the vital organs, then pulled the blade out and, holding it level with the ground, drove it into the remaining attacker's face.

The man's features disappeared in a spray of blood as he stared briefly at the three bodies and turned to seek more of the enemy.

From behind a giant of a man raced past him and flung his battle-ax at the Kalabrian's back and splintered his spine. Desperately Zhuzak tried to tear the embedded weapon from his body, then surrendered and pitched forward.

All around his still body, the fight raged on. Attacker after attacker fell, and still they came, a determined wave of screeching invaders rushing to their deaths.

For every one of Brom's men who fell, a dozen of the enemy died. But the onslaught continued, as though the opponents were trying to hasten their own dying.

For an hour the sounds of metal clanging against metal, men screaming at their own death and the terrified neighing of horses filled the air.

Brom's sword arm was growing weary. He withdrew his krall with his other hand just as an attacker tried to sneak up behind him.

Spinning around, Brom swiftly sliced his throat, then turned away as a fountain of blood spurted from the severed vessels.

Pausing briefly, the Kalabrian leader scanned the battlefield and estimated that more than five hundred men had already been slain or rendered useless. As he looked around, he saw only thirty of his own men still standing. He prayed Zhuzak was one of them, even though he couldn't be seen.

Brom looked up at the butte. Atop his mount, Peytok was waving his sword high in the air.

Responding to his command, a hundred soldiers rushed into the battle from hiding places.

Peytok must have stolen the treasuries of three countries to afford this many professional soldiers, Brom decided angrily.

He looked around for a shimmering cloud, but he couldn't see any signs of one.

There was no time to wonder what had happened. Two combatants, fresh and well rested, were rushing toward him with their swords drawn.

SITTING ON THE BED of his small room at the temple, Hogan started assembling his equipment into the two large duffel bags.

He locked a clip into the seventeen-and-a-half-pound Heckler & Koch PSG1 automatic rifle that handled .308-caliber rounds. With its twenty-five-and-a-half-inch barrel, it was ideal for long distances—especially with the Hemsoldt 6-42X scope. He loaded the other of the two M-16A1 rifles he was taking, then decided to take most of the available ammunition, as well as a dozen of the incendiary and fragmentation grenades in the cases and two dozen palm-sized plastic bombs and timers.

The gun belt with the holstered 9 mm Beretta 92-F, in cock-and-lock position, and the eighteen-inch krall was still lying on the bed.

He decided to add a pair of camouflage coveralls and combat boots, a tool kit, an assortment of electronics gear and a first-aid kit.

A shoulder bag was filled with a dozen ampules of antidote serum for the toxic gas, disposable syringes and two large tubes of ointment to counteract the corrosive action of the gas vapors. A pair of thin, metallic-fabric contamination jumpsuits and masks had also been included.

Hogan surveyed the rest of the gear, and reluctantly he decided that there was no way he could lug the .50-caliber M-60 machine gun with attached tripod, or the four cases of belt-fed ammunition that came with it.

He'd also have to leave behind the quartet of missiles, complete with launcher, that the man in Washington thought might come in handy.

He changed into a fresh pair of jeans and long-sleeved work shirt and slipped his stockinged feet back into his black cowboy boots. Then remembered he had forgotten to pack any clothing.

Gathering up several changes, he shoved them into one of the bags, then grabbed his toothbrush and toothpaste, the old-fashioned Gillette double-edge razor he preferred, his brush and comb and slipped them into the same bag.

Then he strapped the gun belt around his waist.

Now he was ready to find the devil who caused the deaths and send him back to hell.

In Australia was the best clue he had, but it was a very big country and he needed more information so he wouldn't set off on a wild-goose chase.

He sat down on his bed and started to make plans. The American Embassy would have to be his first stop.

Then he realized the dust motes had come to life and were swirling with a golden light in the corner.

The devil would have to wait. Brom needed him.

Grabbing the combo rifle and grenade launcher, the two large duffels and the shoulder bag, Hogan stepped into the center of the glowing mist.

18

Marco paced restlessly before the retired industrialist's large desk as Kalidonian explained Karla Hamilton's plan.

"It's crazy," he snapped. "Ask Dr. Nis."

"Nis is not available," Kalidonian replied.

His adviser had vanished again. The ex-industrialist had become too frightened of the strange man and his mysterious disappearances to dare ask him where he went.

Marco sent a dark look Karla's way. So much had been going wrong. The loss of the teams he had sent after the American, including the North Korean pair who were supposed to be the best. Now Karla's scheme, which could expose them prematurely. She wasn't really one of them. And if he didn't know better, he'd swear she'd found a way to send messages to the outside.

"She's got a video camera," he said in a skeptical voice. "Why can't we tape your speech right here in the biosphere?"

"If we want the networks to run Kalidonian's statement, it has to be on one-inch stock," she lied, sounding calm and professional. "All I have is a video camera that can record on half-inch tape."

Kalidonian interrupted. "When they realize what I am..."

Karla thought fast. "But they won't know that until they view the tape. And if it's not on one inch, they might not bother looking at it." She swallowed hard, then continued. "If you only knew how many tapes television networks are offered."

Marco's face was filled with anger. "She's trying to pull something," he shouted.

Kalidonian studied the German, then in turn, inspected Karla.

She looked aloof and professional.

Kalidonian turned back to Marco. "You can keep an eye on her while we're taping my statement."

Karla stifled a sigh of relief.

"The nearest studio with one-inch equipment is in Darwin," she said.

"We've got more important things to..." Marco snapped, then saw the icy, angry expression on Kalidonian's face and realized what had come out of his mouth. "What I meant—" he said in an altered tone.

"Get a helicopter to take us to Darwin," Kalidonian ordered, punctuating each word deliberately.

Karla Hamilton smiled at him as Marco stared at her. Then, without saying a word Marco stalked out of Kalidonian's office.

HOGAN HAD BEEN transported to Kalabria into the midst of a battle. He saw Brom surrounded by four horsemen. Brom kept slashing his broadsword at his attackers, but as one of them fell, another from behind moved in to take his place.

It was time to get involved, Black Jack decided, seeing the hard pressed warrior. He hastily dropped the bags to the ground and aimed the bulky Colt M-16 A1, loaded with fragmentation grenades, at a cluster of soldiers racing to join the attack on the red-bearded giant.

He dropped one into the center of the pack of mounted men and watched as exploding particles of burning metal cut through their armor as if the hammered-metal plates were made of paper.

Terrified screams tore from the mouths of the men who fell under the stomping feet of their mounts.

Two more were wounded but had managed to stay in their saddles. They looked back at the strange newcomer holding the odd weapon to his shoulder. "The Kalabrian gods are chasing us," one shrieked, ignoring his painful wounds and the gold he had been promised as he urged his horse to carry him from the scene of the battle.

The second stared at Hogan as if he were seeing a monster, then tried to outrun his comrade.

One of Brom's attackers paused briefly to stare at Black Jack, then saw flashing metal as the blade in the red-beard's hand cleaved down through his shoulder blade at an angle and veered across to his heart muscle.

A miniature sea of blood escaped through his severed vessels and drenched him as he mouthed his last curse and fell like a lump of clay at Brom's feet.

Hogan squeezed the trigger and sprayed a short burst of tumblers at a pair of horn-helmeted killers who were hiding in ambush behind a pile of bodies.

Three rounds fired. Three rounds connected.

The men screamed as the lead tore into them, but despite the huge cavities in their midsections, they tried to get to their feet to run.

"Die, dirt," Hogan shouted as he unleashed a second wave to make sure they were dead.

Next Hogan emptied his clip on a mounted group of eight who were gathering to charge him. Three tumbled from their saddles, and another two grabbed at their chests and slumped forward. The remaining three stared at him uncertainly poised between wanting to charge at him and wanting to flee.

Black Jack let the empty clip drop to the ground while he rammed a fresh one in and jacked one into the chamber.

He aimed his M-16 at the remaining three, who turned and rode quickly through a narrow pass between two of the hills.

Hogan cleared a path to the side of the blood-covered Kalabrian leader. A half-dozen dead soldiers later, he was standing beside Brom.

"These are Peytok's hirelings," Brom shouted as he ran his blade through a foot soldier who'd come too close.

"What's left of them," Hogan replied as he washed a cluster of four horn-helmeted men with a shower of fragmenting lead.

Three fell to the ground. The fourth turned and ran, dropping his weapons to gain speed.

Suddenly there was a lull. Hogan knew that, like the eye of a hurricane, a momentary calm in a battle only gave both sides a chance to catch their breath and, possibly, pull some of their dead from the war ground.

Brom and Hogan looked around. Only twenty Kalabrians were still mounted or standing on the ground.

"Where is Zhuzak?" he asked.

Brom shook his head. He didn't know.

As if to answer Hogan's question, a young soldier approached them and beckoned for Brom to follow. Hogan went with them, ever alert to surprise attacks. They stopped at the fallen form of a dying warrior who was gasping for air.

It was Zhuzak, commander of the Kalabrian troops.

Sadness filled Brom's face. This was the bull of the army, reliable, proud and daring. A giant of a man.

The fallen soldier's thick black beard was splattered with blood from the deep gashes in his throat, his face, the shattered skull where a mercenary's battle-ax had splintered the thick bone.

The Kalabrian ruler knelt beside him, then looked up. Hogan could see the tears that Brom refused to shed gather in the corners of his eyes.

Black Jack knelt beside him and watched as Brom cradled the dying man in his arms.

Zhuzak opened his eyes and smiled when he saw Hogan.

"Well, *Dula,* our next wrestling match will be in another place."

Once he had used the word insultingly, calling Hogan a "little boy" but after they had settled their differences, it had become a term of earned affection and respect.

"You're just looking for an easy way to avoid fighting me," Black Jack said gruffly.

Zhuzak lifted his right hand into the air.

"One last arm wrestle," he pleaded.

"Later."

"I've always wanted to die fighting."

Hogan and Brom exchanged glances, then the American lightly grasped the dying man's huge hand.

Zhuzak closed his hand around Hogan's and tried to force it down. Hogan started to let him win.

"Fight back like a man," Zhuzak gasped.

"Do it, Hogan," Brom ordered, and reluctantly Hogan forced the weakened arm to the ground.

Zhuzak grinned fiercely.

"There will be another time," he promised in a whisper. Then he reached out and wrapped his other hand around the short sword lying near him.

Still smiling defiantly, he closed his eyes and became still.

Black Jack felt the wetness from his eyes brush across his cheeks, then looked at Brom, who wept openly.

Hogan had lost a friend and Brom a comrade.

Two of the enemy violated the unwritten rules of battle and tried to ambush them during the lull. In a rage of anger, the brothers-in-arms sensed their presence and turned.

Brom swung his sword with all his might at one of the attacking pair and separated his body into two parts.

Hogan didn't wait to watch. He dropped his automatic and, furious at Zhuzak's death, grabbed a fallen battle-ax and threw it.

The weapon delivered a blow to the attacker that removed him from the ranks of the living, with barely enough time to allow him a last strangled cry.

Just then the sound of a horn, pierced through the air. Hogan and Brom looked up and saw Peytok next to a soldier sounding a sheep's horn. Peytok beckoned to his surviving men below, then disappeared over the hill in a cloud of dust.

Grabbing riderless horses, Peytok's men mounted them and sped toward the pass next to the butte in a headless rush.

Brom shouted out a command. "On your horses and after them!"

He grabbed the reins of his mount and clambered onto the saddle.

"Wait for me," Hogan yelled.

Brom hesitated, then turned and saw the last of his men, already swallowed up by the pass.

"Follow us," he said, riding full speed ahead.

Hogan dashed to where he'd dropped his bags. As he looked around for a horse, something caught his eye from a distance.

He saw an enemy soldier standing on the butte opposite the one the Nordian ruler had climbed. He held something in his hand.

Black Jack recognized it, even as he fought a sensation of disbelief.

It was a canister of poison gas.

This had been a trap, and Brom had rushed into it.

There was no time to reach the Kalabrian, so he tried shouting. "It's a trap."

Brom stopped his animal and turned back. He waved to Hogan encouragingly, then spurred his horse into the pass.

Hogan fell to his knees and tore open one of the bags.

Retrieving the already armed Heckler & Koch PSG1, he quickly pulled the tripod legs open and set it on the ground, then focused through the powerful scope mounted on it.

He could see the soldier through the telescope.

Black Jack glanced down to make sure there was a clip in the weapon, then forced his eye against the scope again.

Moving his weapon a fraction, he had the mercenary's chest lined up with the cross hairs.

He pulled the trigger.

The .308 Remington left the muzzle at a velocity of 3770 feet per second. Through the glass he saw the lead's trajectory as it sped to the butte and sliced into the chest of the lone figure.

As he watched, the wounded man tottered, only to fall backward and disappear still clutching the gas canister.

"No!" Hogan cried out as he grabbed his shoulder bag and seized the reins of a horse.

As he jumped into the saddle and took off, his hair flying wildly about him, he prayed he wouldn't be too late to save Brom.

19

After the helicopter ride, the hired limousine had driven them from the airport to the modern two-story structure that housed Outback Post Productions, Ltd., on the outskirts of Darwin.

With Kalidonian and Marco listening, Karla Hamilton had called ahead from the biosphere and asked for the managing director. She had been put through to Harvey Penbrooke by an awed receptionist who recognized her name. Penbrooke had been impressed by her name and reputation and offered her full cooperation.

So that part of her plan went well, but the hardest part still lay ahead. As they walked through the front doors, Marco wrapped one of his hands around her wrists.

"Give me any reasons for suspicion, and you will die," he whispered. "I haven't got anything to lose."

She looked at him, and knew he wasn't just threatening. She had been a witness to the death of the Thai villagers and to his bragging that he had been responsible for organizing the event.

"I'm trying to do the right thing for Kalidonian," she said coolly, trying to hide the terror she felt inside.

A young blond woman jumped up from behind the reception desk when she saw Karla approaching.

"You're really Karla Hamilton," she said enthusiastically as she grabbed the newscaster's hand and shook it. "I'm Penny Simpson. I thought one of my mates was treating me like a 'galah'..." She saw the puzzled expression on Karla's face. "It means a fool," she explained. Then she got enthusiastic again. "But it's really you. Wait till I tell old Harv."

One of the doors swung open, and an energetic-looking man in jeans and opened-necked button-down shirt entered the reception area.

He smiled patiently at the blonde and asked, "Tell old Harv what?"

"It's her," Penny said, pointing to the brunette. "Karla Hamilton."

"I know. My eyes work, Penny." He turned to Karla and extended a hand. "Welcome to Outback Post Productions, Miss Hamilton. I'm Harv—" he smiled and caught himself "—Harvey Penbrooke."

He turned and studied Kalidonian until Marco stepped between them.

With a snarl, Marco asked, "Something bothering you?"

Ignoring him, Penbrooke maintained his steady regard. "I know you," he finally said. "You're the chap who built that bloody biosphere out there in the outback near Alice Springs."

The short stout man held out a hand. "Argun Kalidonian."

The two men shook hands.

Then Penbrooke switched his attention to Karla, again.

"I think I know what you want," he said.

Marco stiffened. Karla saw his hardened expression, and to stop him from speaking, hurriedly said, "I need to tape a statement from Mr. Kalidonian about the biosphere and what will happen if..."

Kalidonian stepped in. "Let's not give everything away, or there will be nothing left for the television networks to broadcast," he said, but there was a warning in his voice.

"Yes, of course," Karla replied quickly. To Penbrooke she said, "If you'll set up the camera and one-inch tape machine, I can operate both."

"You sure you don't want my men to help you?" He looked confused. "They come with the room."

"We want to keep my statement confidential until the day we are ready to release it," Kalidonian explained calmly.

"However, we will need at least four copies of the tape," Karla added, and looked at Kalidonian for approval.

"If you say so, my dear," he answered, suddenly sounding relaxed.

"Let me show you what we've set up in our studio." Penbrooke then led the three visitors to a corridor.

He called back to the receptionist. "Find out what everyone wants to drink, Penny. Then be a good girl and get it for them."

A LIBRARY SET had been erected in the small television studio. Tall bookcases filled with the facades of books stood behind a large burly maple desk.

"Do you want the microphone to show, or should we use a lapel mike?"

Karla was just about to ask Kalidonian, then made the decision herself. "Let the microphone show."

"How about the cameras? We can slave them so you can tape him from every angle with one control, then edit the statement afterward."

The former industrialist was very familiar with video techniques from exposure to them through his various advertising directors. "I prefer that there be no editing." He turned to Karla. "We will tape it head-on."

"Then you'll be set to go in a few minutes, mates."

Penny entered the room carrying a tray.

"Meantime, here's the soft drinks you ordered," Penbrooke said heartily. He paused and looked at Marco. "Sure you wouldn't like something stronger, like a Fosters?"

Marco shook his head and reached for the glass of bottled water.

"Better round up some men to help me get set up," Penbrooke said, and left the studio.

Karla stepped up to the receptionist. "Is there a ladies' room nearby?"

"Just around the corner. Come on. I'll show you."

Karla started to follow Penny out of the studio, but Marco stopped her at the doorway.

She stared him down. "Would you like to come with me to the bathroom?"

Marco turned to Kalidonian for instructions. "Let her go. Just keep an eye on the door to the bathroom."

Karla Hamilton clutched her purse tightly. Inside was the exposed film. Somehow she had to find a way to get it to John Hogan, without being seen passing it on.

HOGAN WASN'T INTERESTED in anything except the still, redbearded body that had fallen from the saddle to the ground.

He had quickly pulled on the contamination suit and mask. His dying from the gas vapor wouldn't contribute to saving Brom.

Then he remembered Hiram Wilson's words when he handed him the ampules of antidote and the contamination gear: *The ass you save may be your own.*

If Mondlock was right about their fates being intertwined, saving Brom was the same as saving himself.

Kneeling beside Brom, Black Jack filled a syringe with the antidote and injected it. Then he pulled off the Kalabrian's shirt and searched for some indication of how much gas Brom had been exposed to.

There were a number of places where his skin had become red and angry, but none had erupted into open sores.

Hogan opened a tube of ointment and slathered the warrior's face and body with it. Then he grabbed his M-16, the shoulder bag of antidotes, got up and looked around for other survivors.

Twenty Kalabrians had died in the narrow pass along with their horses.

Their faces and bodies were covered with weeping wounds from the corrosive gas vapors. None of them could be saved, Hogan decided sadly.

At the far end of the pass Hogan spotted a couple more bodies, and he worked his way to them.

The mercenary who had released the vapor was dead. So was his horse.

Next to them there was a khaki-colored canister on the ground. Black Jack glanced at the stenciled words. They were the same as those on the other canisters he'd seen. The logo of the American government. It seemed strange to see it on this different world, and almost impossible. But Hogan knew that he and Brom were not the only ones who could move between the two worlds.

Beyond the pass, he saw a large group of armed men. In their midst the ruler Brom had called Peytok was sitting on his horse, arguing with another man who stood on the ground, his back to the pass.

There was something uncomfortably familiar about the way the standing man shifted his body and held his head. Hogan wanted to get a look at his face.

Then, as the figure turned slightly, he saw his features and recognized the bright blond hair and almond-shaped eyes.

It was the creature Nis.

Hogan lifted his M-16 combo to his shoulder to fire, then realized he'd just waste his ammunition and call needless attention to himself. In his previous face-to-face encounter with Nis, he'd seen the bullets pass straight through his body without harming him.

He'd have to let Mondlock or Mok Seng come up with a way to destroy him.

Meantime, he had to get Brom back to Tella. And back to life, if that was still possible.

He moved quickly to the fallen warrior and lifted his massive body. Sweating from the weight, Black Jack slung the still form across the front of his saddle. Then he climbed up and mounted.

He rode the large animal through the battlefield of death, pausing to retrieve his two duffel bags, then mercilessly spurred his horse to start galloping faster with the double load than he had ever run.

A man's life was at stake. Brom's.

No, he corrected himself. Two lives were at stake, if Mondlock was right. Brom's life—and his own.

He couldn't admit that the red-bearded warrior might be dead. The two of them were too stubborn to give up so easily, he kept reminding himself as he continued to ride hard toward Tella.

KARLA SAT inside the stall, behind a closed door, staring at the three rolls of film from her Minox camera she had hidden in her handbag. How was she going to get them delivered to John Hogan, the one man she believed could help?

Outside, the young receptionist kept chattering away in front of the mirror.

"Wait till I tell my girlfriends that I met Karla Hamilton. They'll die of jealousy," she gushed.

Karla was tempted to entrust the task of getting the film delivered to the American Embassy to Penny. The Embassy could forward them to the American agent, she was certain. Trouble was, she wasn't too sure that the seemingly flighty Penny Simpson could be trusted with the task, especially when it could end up endangering her, as well.

Karla stood and started to drop the films back in her bag. She'd have to find another way, she thought, then realized this might be the only opportunity she would have before the planned announcement date.

She'd have to convince the receptionist quickly, or Marco would burst into the ladies' room to see what was taking her so long, no matter how his actions appeared to the others.

Karla opened the door.

"You're done," the young girl said brightly.

"Penny, I need a favor. A *big* favor."

"Anything you want, Miss Hamilton. Name it."

"Can you keep a secret?"

"You ask my girlfriend Helene about the time she came home and found out she was pregnant and begged me not to tell her folks. They never heard about it from me, not even after they told her to get married or get out. Why, I probably know more about what old Harv does than his wife—"

"I haven't got much time," Karla interrupted.

"Sorry. Sometimes I don't know when to stop talking."

Karla opened her bag and took out the tiny cassettes of film. "Can you memorize some things?"

"I've got a great memory. You ask Harv Penbrooke how many times I've remembered—"

"I want you to get these films to the American Embassy."

"In Sydney?"

"No. The American government has a consulate in Darwin."

"If you want, I can call a messenger and have them get it right over."

"No!" Karla was getting frustrated. "Wait until after we leave. Then take it there yourself. Ask for the consul and let him know that these films have to get in the hands of John Hogan."

"If he works there, why don't I just give them to him?"

"He doesn't work there. He works... It doesn't matter. Tell the consul John Hogan lives in a Buddhist temple in the Angkor Wat ruins. The films contain information that he must have immediately. Tell him to let John Hogan know that I took the pictures."

"I'll stop there on my way home," Penny promised. "Do you want me to repeat the information?" Without waiting, she started to recite Karla's words. "Tell the consul these films have to get in the hands of John Hogan who lives in a Buddhist..."

There was an angry hammering on the door. Marco's voice boomed through the thick wood.

"Karla, Mr. Kalidonian is very anxious to get started— now!"

Karla nervously ran her fingers through her hair and began to open the door. Then she stopped and looked at the blond receptionist.

"This is our secret. Not a word to anyone."

Penny grinned. "Except for the American consul. Right?"

Karla sighed. "Right."

Then she opened the door.

Marco examined her suspiciously, then stared at Penny with cold, observant eyes.

Finally he spoke to Karla. "What took you so long?"

Karla faked embarrassment. "I had to change something." She hesitated. "It's that time of the month."

He opened and closed his fists as he weighed her reply, then he grabbed her and started to pull her down the corridor.

"Don't worry, Miss Hamilton. I'll make sure . . ."

Karla looked back at Penny, her eyes filled with pleading. Her body became tense.

Penny Simpson caught herself. "I'll make sure no one disturbs you while you're taping."

Karla Hamilton's body relaxed, and she thought she was going to faint with relief.

But immediately another thought entered her mind. What if the American consul didn't believe Penny?

THE FOUR OF THEM had been gathered around the large bed for most of the night.

Black Jack Hogan sat on a wooden footstool, his eyes fixed unwaveringly on Brom. But Brom hadn't moved a muscle.

During the vigil Hogan had injected another ampule of the antitoxin and again soothed the Kalabrian ruler's reddened body and face with the special ointment provided by Hiram Wilson.

So far there had been no visible results.

Mora was kneeling at the side of the bed. Her pale blond hair veiled her face, and her body was shaken by tiny tremors. She seemed to be in a state of shock, too stunned to speak and too heartsick to move.

Astrah was beside her, smoothing her hair and occasionally whispering in her ear, but Mora was deaf to her words.

Only Mondlock had been mobile, spending time in the royal chamber checking the condition of the Kalabrian leader, then leaving for an hour.

Hogan took his eyes from the unmoving form on the bed and watched the Knower come back into the sleeping chamber. His tired mind conjured up fearful plots, and he felt even Mondlock couldn't be trusted. What was the old man scheming while Brom was in no position to protest? Filled with suspicion Hogan asked, "Where did you go?"

"The same place I had gone to the other times I left."

"Where is that?"

"The chapel of the gods to join with the other priests in prayer."

Hogan understood and felt jealous. He had no relationship like the one between Brom and Mondlock. Then he thought of Mok Seng, and realized he did.

He glanced back to where his friend...no, he changed the word...his twin lay.

Would Brom ever return from the coma of the poison gas?

He got his answer moments later when the head resting on the pillows moved.

Mora lifted her head and watched while tears ran down her cheeks. Astrah, beside her, cried openly.

Black Jack stole a glance at the usually impassive wise man. Mondlock's eyes were wet and red.

Slowly Brom's eyes opened, and he looked at each of the four around his bed.

In a harsh whisper he asked, "Has someone died?"

"No," Mora replied with a tremulous smile. "Someone has come back to life."

She reached out and held his hand, still limp and weak.

The warrior groaned. "I feel like somebody has pounded inside my head and body with a heavy hammer," he complained.

"They did," Hogan replied. "Only it was invisible."

Brom blinked his eyes. "The vapor?"

"One of Peytok's men released it as you entered the pass."

The Kalabrian hesitated, then asked, "The others?"

"Dead. As are most of the attackers. They received a full dose. You were lucky enough to only be touched by a small amount."

Brom's voice was suddenly filled with sadness. "Where is Zhuzak's body?"

Mondlock spoke. "It was brought back to Tella with the bodies of the other warriors for preparation."

"I wanted to light his funeral pyre," Brom said quietly. He looked at Mondlock.

"You shall. It was decided to delay the ceremonies until..." He stopped, unwilling to finish the sentence. *Until you had died* were the words he left out.

Brom next questioned Hogan. "Did Peytok die?"

"No, but he will," Hogan promised.

As weak as he was, the Kalabrian warrior's voice was filled with rage and promise. "Not until I am strong enough to help kill him."

Mora, who had been clutching Brom's hand, finally got her emotions under control. "Peytok can wait. And you need your rest," she said in a crisp, commanding voice.

She reached down and opened the soft leather bag on the floor. From inside she took out vials of ointments, liquids and folded pads of cloth. She wet the pads with one of the liquids, then gently wiped the sick man's face with them.

"They're cold."

"They will refresh you."

The Kalabrian stopped complaining. He knew Mora was a trained healer. Her father had been Dorisan, a high priest and healer. Having no son, he had taught her how to use the herbs and medicines that healed the sick and wounded.

Brom glanced at her as she saturated another pad.

She was wearing a loose tunic of thin material, and wide-legged pants of colored fibers. As she leaned over him, the front of her tunic opened, and he caught a glimpse of her small, firm breasts. The sweet smell of her body made his nostrils flare.

She was wearing no coverings under her outer garments. Brom cursed the enemy who had made him unable to enjoy her.

She saw where his eyes were focused and smiled.

"There will be many evenings after you have regained your strength," she whispered.

Hogan stretched his legs and got to his feet.

"It's time for me to return to my world and start searching," he announced. "The source of the gas is there."

Astrah rose from her knees and moved to his side.

"An hour or two won't matter."

Black Jack was about to argue, then changed his mind as he looked into her soft, small face. Besides, time seemed different in its flow when he was in Kalabria, since it did not appear to match Earth time in duration.

Her eyes promised so much, and he would need all the joy he could remember in the days ahead.

He let her lead him toward the door.

"If you light the funeral fires before I return, tell Zhuzak's spirit I expect a decent wrestling match the next time we meet," he called out to Brom.

"The gods willing," Astrah said to him in a low voice, "you will be too old and worn from our times alone for combat when that happens."

Hogan hoped she was right. But he felt the chill of the battles he knew were still ahead as he followed the small maiden with hair the color of wild strawberries out of the bed chamber.

20

Karla Hamilton was lost in her thoughts. She glanced out of the helicopter's small window at the stark landscape of the outback, wondering if the films would reach John Hogan in time for him to stop Kalidonian and his henchmen.

Below her she saw savage beauty.

The thick shrubbery of the Top End, as the Australians called the upper half of the outback, was largely a subtropical jungle, populated by crocodiles and snakes, as well as graceful animals and birds.

She looked to the west and stared at Butterfly Gorge, a breathtaking, deep crevice in the surface of the Earth, south of Darwin. Filled with a cornucopia of butterfly species, the area was a haven for a hundred different kinds of birds.

As she watched, a huge mass of birds flew toward the sky, filling the air with a chorale of avian music. Magpie geese, plumed whistling ducks, plovers, as well as jabirus and brulgas moved their wings gracefully as they soared above the helicopter.

The landscape swiftly changed before her eyes as they reached the area the natives called the Red Centre. By contrast to the Top End, the Red Centre was an endless span of sunbaked land.

Karla stared down at the parched land to search for signs of life. Only miles of spinifex grass and dry mulga scrub relieved the monotony.

Toward the south she saw a huge flat-topped red mountain rising straight up from the desertlike floor.

This was Ayers Rock—the largest isolated rock in the world. It stood 1100 feet above the plains and was six miles in circumference.

Fourteen miles to the west stood the thirty-six stone domes of the Olgas Range, filled with caves and hidden pools of water that had sustained the nearby aborigines for the forty thousand years scientists estimated they had inhabited the outback.

Karla forced her eyes from the window, then leaned back in her seat and closed them.

The aborigines and the others who lived in and around the outback would become a vanished species if Hogan couldn't stop Kalidonian from executing his ultimate plan.

Northern Australia was one of the targets on the list she had found in Marco's room.

Suddenly she heard Kalidonian's voice. "You seem very quiet," he said.

Karla opened her eyes and looked at him. "Just resting. Taping is hard work."

"I found it very pleasant," he replied, fondling the four boxes that contained the original and copies of his statement. "Thanks to you, my dear, I am almost ready to release these tapes to the television networks."

"Almost?" The surprised voice that asked the question belonged to Marco, who was sitting behind Karla Hamilton.

Kalidonian turned his head back.

"We need to bring the rest of the shells from the island warehouse into the biosphere first." Then he paused. "And there is one more thing you need to do."

The brunette sat up and listened. This might be important new information she should memorize.

"We need to tighten our security," Kalidonian said softly, nodding at Karla.

She was wondering what he meant when Marco said, "I understand. I brought one of my pens."

He took a ballpoint out of a jacket pocket and exposed the recessed point. Karla heard the soft click and turned to see what had caused it.

Marco jabbed her forearm with the point.

She was about to ask why he had done such a stupid thing when she felt numbness race through her body.

A great, certain knowledge flooded her brain—the knowledge that she was dying.

If she only could contact the American consul and tell him what had just happened. But suddenly it didn't matter. Nothing did, and she slumped forward in her seat.

WILSON COULDN'T tear his eyes away from the enlargements of the photographs the security laboratory had hand delivered to him and whistled. There was more than enough evidence of murder and other crimes to convict Kalidonian and the others in the biosphere.

The white-haired man was stunned. He would never have suspected the former industrialist of being behind the theft of the toxic gas shells and canisters.

He still didn't understand why the extremely wealthy man had done it. But frequently the motives of madmen still eluded him.

Kalidonian's history was no mystery. Wilson had had the CIA put together a dossier on him.

With the knowledge he had gained from the photographs, he could trace the chronology of events.

The death by accidental gas poisoning of the industrialist's son and family. His sudden interest in environmental affairs—more manic than those who tried to effect change through laws and persuasion. The announcement of the plans to construct a huge biosphere in the outback of Australia. The recruiting of volunteers to populate the controlled-environment community and the new information that all of them were known or suspected terrorists.

Except for the woman who had sent the film.

Karla Hamilton was a respected journalist. Somewhat theatrical in her need to find major news scoops, but nonetheless a hard-working investigative reporter.

Hiram Wilson couldn't imagine why she got involved with Kalidonian—unless she smelled a big story and wanted to break it first.

He was grateful she had decided the survival of the world was more important than scoop, and that the American consul in Darwin took immediate action to have the films addressed to Black Jack flown to Washington by military jet.

The decision he had to make was how to act on this information.

He had tried to find his agent but, found no trace of him. Probably he was searching for leads to the location of the shells.

Wilson picked up one of the photographs. The names and places on the handwritten list were legible. These were the places Kalidonian's agents had planted the gas dispensers.

At least most of them.

What concerned the President's aide was where the rest of the pirated cargo was.

He had considered a joint Australian-American assault on the biosphere but had changed his mind.

Premature action could lead to retaliation by Kalidonian's henchmen—retaliation in the form of the missing shells and canisters.

Somebody had to find out the storage site.

The only one he would trust to do that was Black Jack Hogan, who had dropped from sight.

Wilson made a decision.

He lifted the phone. "Get me that Buddhist monk in Cambodia," he told his secretary. "I want to leave an urgent message for Black Jack."

ASTRAH KISSED Hogan farewell and watched as he vanished into the shimmering cloud, bags and all.

Then she sought out Mora.

"He's gone," she said sadly.

"He'll return."

"Why did he have to leave?"

"Like Lord Brom, he has answers to find and his destiny to fulfill."

"I do not understand why men like Lord Brom and Hogan are so occupied with fighting."

"That is the way they prevent those who would destroy us from winning. That is his destiny, as it is Lord Brom's. It has been so since both of them returned from the dead."

Astrah was confused. "You spoke of this before. But when I was a temple maiden and assisted the priests, the dead never returned."

"They weren't Lord Brom. Or Hogan. I do not completely understand it, but Mondlock says that both had virtually died and that in returning to life their spirits were merged."

"So their destinies are bound together," Astrah commented.

"For eternity. Or as long as both of them shall live."

Astrah's face darkened. "Hogan better live for a long time. I have plans for him."

Mora laughed and put an arm around her waist. "Well, that is just fine, but don't tell him. Men—even brave warriors—grow weak and frightened at such simple truths."

21

Wilson's signal, reported by Mok Seng when Hogan contacted the temple, had urged him to call Washington in a hurry. The Intelligence aide reviewed the information in the photographs.

"So you are already in Australia. Good work. The woman who smuggled the films out to us is inside the biosphere."

"No, she's not," Hogan reported. "A ranger found what was left of her body in the desert. A pack of hungry dingoes had dug up the shallow grave. Before the ranger could scare them off, they had started devouring her remains."

Both of them were silent for a moment, then Wilson reminded Hogan that their first concern was with the missing shells and canisters.

"Take care, Black Jack," Wilson ordered. "You'd be hard to replace." With that comforting thought, Hogan went to his destination.

Now he sat in the jeep he had picked up in Darwin. Looming ahead of him was the vast hemispheric dome. He had brought the equipment of war with him because there was no way of knowing what he might need to complete this mission. Right now all of it seemed useless.

Inside the structure was the man he had sought, along with his associates. They were all there, except those who were waiting for a signal in more than twenty cities around the world.

And they were safe from any actions by him—unless he wanted to sacrifice millions of innocent lives to destroy them. His head was filled with dark thoughts when a voice interrupted his thinking.

"Looks like you've got a problem, mate."

Hogan turned and looked at the small, dark-skinned man dressed in tattered Western-style clothing.

"Where'd you come from?"

"Been here long before you arrived. Thousands of years, in fact, mate."

Despite his feelings of frustration, Black Jack smiled.

The small man was right. He and his ancestors had occupied this land long before the British had brought their convicts here to populate it.

The man spoke up again.

"Got any tucker with you?"

"Tucker?"

The man laughed with glee. "Forgot you were a Yank. Tucker's food. Got anything to eat?"

Black Jack nodded and opened a bag. He'd packed some freeze-dried food. Casually he handed over two packets.

"Military grub," the man sniffed in disdain. "Oh, well, might wash down okay with a cup of billy tea."

He started to walk away. Hogan looked after him. "Where are you going?"

"Need some water to cook this stuff and to brew tea," the other replied as he disappeared behind a large pile of rocks.

Moments later he returned with a full canteen and an armful of dried spinifex grass and some wood. Carefully he pressed some of the grass together and lit it with a match, then waited and fed the flames with pieces of wood.

Soon a large fire was burning, but there was another request to come.

"Got a pot?"

Hogan shook his head.

"Don't matter none."

The aborigine knelt down and removed a hubcap.

"This'll do," he said, carrying the hubcap to the fire and propping it up so it was over the flames.

Carefully he filled it with water, then cut a slit in the freeze-dried packet and spooned food into the boiling water and watched as the two packets heated. Then he lifted them gingerly and handed them to the American.

"Careful, mate. It's hot."

After they had eaten, the two men sipped the strangely flavored tea from cups Black Jack had found in his gear.

He studied the aborigine again.

"Got a name?"

"Folks called me Nipper Tokubba. I'm Pitjantjatjara."

Hogan knew the word. He had been briefed quickly in Darwin by one of the Australian security police about the aborigine tribes.

"I thought aborigines went naked except for a loin-cloth."

"They do. I've been working as a hand at a cattle station until day before yesterday."

"You quit?"

Nipper nodded. "To come help you."

Hogan hid his surprise. He had only arrived in Darwin thirty hours ago. "How'd you know I was coming?"

"Heard."

One of the things he'd been warned by the briefing officers was not to try to push the aborigines for explanations. They clammed up quickly.

Hogan changed his tactics. "How can you help me?"

"You wanna get inside that thing."

The American stopped wondering how the man named Nipper knew. He just nodded his head.

"But you're worried they'll get even if you do."

Hogan felt as though he was talking to a dark-skinned version of Mok Seng or Mondlock.

"Yes."

"No worry, mate. They been hauling stuff here by helicopter for days. Looks like everything they were shipping is inside. The sky birds stopped coming this morning."

The American agent wasn't sure he could risk so much on the word of one man. Even someone like Nipper.

He got to his feet and walked to his jeep. Then he opened a metal box. Inside was a poison-gas canister he had finally convinced Wilson he needed.

Nipper was already standing behind him, and got an eyeful.

"Any of them look like this?" Hogan questioned.

"Some. Rest of them were different."

Black Jack hadn't brought a picture of the shells, so he had to rely on description. "How do the rest look?"

"Like tank shells."

At Hogan's inquiring look, Nipper grinned. "Handled enough of them during the Second World War when I was in the army."

"Oh," Hogan said as he stared at the man. He didn't know what else to say.

"Don't let it grab you, mate. I don't understand how I do it, either. So we're even."

"Why are you offering to help me?"

"Them inside killed a lot of my mates the other day. I tried a bunch of Pitjantjatjara magic, but they don't seem to work against that thing," Nipper said, pointing to the biosphere. "Even got me a Kaditja man—that's a tribal executioner—to come out and do his thing on them. Didn't do no good. So when I knew you were coming and why you were here, figured you might need a hand."

"First thing I must do is get inside."

"There ain't no way, mate. They got the bloody place sealed up like a coffin. I tried to get some of the sliding metal panels open, but they're locked from the inside."

"I might need to contact the Australian air force to come and bomb the biosphere."

"No need to do that. Got any explosives?"

Hogan thought of the plastic explosives he had brought. "Yes."

"They got a weak spot. A big unit that takes out the stale air and cleans the air coming in through a mess of filters. It's up there on top of the round ball," the small man said, pointing to the top of the biosphere. "Blow that up, and sooner or later they're going to have to come out and fix it."

"They must have an interior air-circulating system," Black Jack commented.

"They got that, all right. Kin of mine, a bright kid named Tommy Makkarouba, who was studying engineering up at that university in Darwin, helped build this thing. He said they could last for three months living off the equipment they got inside." He paused. "He's one of the ones they killed," he added with a hint of bitterness.

Hogan started to develop a plan in his head. He needed some more information.

"You happen to know if there are filters in the unit on the top of the biosphere?"

"They got filters on everything," Nipper replied.

Black Jack was stymied. The biosphere was impenetrable.

"'Course you use enough explosives, you're gonna blow a hole in the roof," Nipper added.

Hogan wasn't about to take any chances. He pressed three of the rough balls of plastic explosives together, then connected a timer to them.

Now he had to figure how he was going to climb up to the unit.

Nipper seemed to read his mind with his answer.

"We got a natural climbing gift. If you set the timer, I'll get it up there."

Hogan frowned. The job was his, and it was dangerous. He wasn't about to pass it on to somebody else.

Nipper could sense his hesitation and quickly understood the reason for it.

"Okay, I'll lead you up there."

When Hogan agreed, Nipper added a suggestion. "If it was me, I'd take that big can you got in the box up with me."

Hogan stared at him.

"And do what with it?"

"Give them back a taste of their own."

The American agent wasn't sure. Retrieving the poison gas was one thing. Killing a community was something else.

"Would them what's inside stop and worry about folks outside if the shoe was on their foot?"

Hogan remembered the villages in Thailand and Kalabria. And the near death of his twin.

From what he'd read about Argun Kalidonian, the old man had seemed sincere about wanting to save the environment. How could good intentions have turned into insanity?

Black Jack didn't have time to worry about it now. Right now there was a world that needed saving from its madmen.

He walked to the jeep and picked up the metal case, then stopped and opened one of his bags.

There were a pair of contamination suits and masks inside. He took them out and handed one to Nipper.

"Put this on."

"Gonna make it harder to climb," he warned.

"There's no other way. You either wear it, or you have to leave the area."

Nipper's response was to slide his body inside the thin, metallic fabric jumpsuit and work his bare feet into the attached boots. Hogan did the same thing. Then he adjusted his own mask and Nipper's also.

His voice sounded muffled as he asked, "Ready?"

"Ready, mate," came the muffled reply.

THE METAL CASE strapped to his back threatened to pull Hogan away from the curved glass-and-metal surface of the biosphere as he imitated the moves of the man ahead of him and slowly worked his way to the top of the structure.

Inch by inch the two men found small edges to grasp with their gloved fingertips, and used them to haul themselves up.

Strapped to Hogan's waist was the plastic explosive and timer. He had fixed another timer to the dispenser on the canister.

His fingers had become cramped and stiff from the excruciatingly slow movement. He kept sliding back, grabbing on an outcropping of metal to stop his fall, then working his way upward again.

The land lay in stillness below them, and the heat waves seemed to condense and spiral in clumps.

Hogan looked away, thinking that the climb and the heat were getting to him.

Ahead of him the small figure in the contamination gear had just reached the top of the dome.

Hogan could feel his strength failing, but he gritted his teeth and commanded his fingers to continue working.

He had managed to almost complete the journey, then looked up and saw a hand reach down to him.

Gratefully he grasped it and let Nipper help him fight his way to the top.

For a moment he sat and rested to catch his breath.

In all the vast emptiness of the outback, there was nothing in sight except for a few plants.

Nipper leaned over to him. "They're all watching us."

"Who?"

"Them what's long gone and them what's still alive."

Black Jack wasn't sure he completely understood what Nipper was trying to tell him.

His reply was muffled. "I hope those who are still alive are pretty far from here."

"They are. I warned them to go."

Hogan turned his head and looked at Nipper through his visored mask.

"When?"

"When we were looking at the canister."

The American didn't pretend to know how the aborigine had done it. But, somehow, he was sure he had.

It was time, he decided, as he felt his strength return.

He opened his suit and took out the plastic explosive, then sealed the contamination uniform.

Carefully he attached the puttylike material to the surface of the biosphere at the point where tubes from the external air-cleansing unit entered the structure.

He started to set the clock for thirty minutes, but Nipper interrupted.

"Make it fifteen," he said through his mask. "We should be down and off by then."

Hogan took his advice. His next step was to unstrap the metal case and take out the canister. He strapped the mouth of the metal unit to the tubes and set the timer on it.

He turned to his companion. "Ready?"

"Any time you are."

Hogan activated the timers, then shouted, "Now!"

The two men worked their way down the outer structure as if they were in a race, but still grabbing the metal holds carefully on their rapid journey to the ground.

As Hogan ran for the jeep, he realized Nipper wasn't with him.

He turned and saw the aborigine moving toward the hills that rose in the distance. He had removed the mask.

Black Jack did the same, then shouted a question, "Where are you going?"

Nipper stopped and turned around. "To tell my mates we might be around for a few more thousand years, thanks to you," Nipper shouted. Then he waved a hand at Hogan and continued on.

Hogan replaced the mask, and keeping his eye on his watch he commenced a countdown.

PEOPLE IN THE BIOSPHERE were going about their business, calm but expectant, when an explosion echoed through it. Kalidonian came rushing out of his office to see what had happened.

Marco Gussman was standing in the center square looking up at the small hole in the roof.

Kalidonian tugged at his arm anxiously. "What happened?"

Marco started to reply, then stopped and grabbed his throat with both hands.

A brief pandemonium set in as men and women started running out into the center courtyard from every direction, gasping for breath and screaming for help.

Kalidonian was shocked. His face and neck felt as though someone had blowtorched them and he tried to rub the burning from his eyes.

Suddenly he realized what had happened. Somebody had released poison gas in the biosphere.

He started to shout a command, but words wouldn't come. All he could think of was that an unseen hand had dared put an end to his noble experiment.

Still trying to call for assistance, he crumpled to the ground. Beside him was Marco's motionless form, and all around, a great silence started to claim the biosphere.

22

Inside the large tent that had become his headquarters in this primitive world, Nis couldn't contain his frustration. His supply of energy had become dangerously low. It was becoming difficult for him to maintain control over his hirelings or the clarity of the human image he had created to function in the two worlds.

Now his desperate search for the vital glowing rocks had been threatened. Especially with the death of Kalidonian and Marco, whom he had designated to spearhead his search in the other world.

The creature called Hogan had retrieved the pirated inventory of shells and canisters from within the biosphere and had dispatched others to retrieve them from their hiding places in the target cities.

What was left was the pathetic creature called Peytok, his handful of mercenaries and one canister of the gas.

If he vanished as the others of his species had, there would be no Guardians, and the other worlds would have to find their own destinies without his guidance and control. Order in the universe would die along with the Guardians.

He tried to reformulate his plans, but thinking required using his supply of energy. He would have to come up with a solution in this world—this primitive world in which the creature called Brom lived.

He had the germ of a plan, although the details would have to wait until he rested. But the plan had real promise, he already saw.

HIRAM WILSON had wanted Hogan to write a full report on exactly what had happened in Australia. The results were obvious, the deaths of Kalidonian and the terrorists who had inhabited the remote biosphere.

But the President had asked him for details on exactly how the agent whose code name was Black Jack had accomplished the almost-impossible feat single-handedly.

Wilson's radio-telephone calls to the temple had gotten him the same response every time.

"Hogan has gone on holiday."

Wilson had alerted Intelligence allies to find the former counterinsurgency specialist. So far no one had been successful.

The phone in his office rang, and when he picked it up, Mrs. Bolivar crisply informed him that it was the man in the Oval Office wanting to know when he could expect the report on the biosphere attack.

Wilson's mind went into high gear as he debated how he could satisfy the President until Hogan reappeared.

BLACK JACK HOGAN sat on a cushion next to Brom inside the huge banquet hall and joined in the prewedding festivities.

The shimmering cloud had transported him and his equipment from Australia to Tella. He barely had time to change before he was summoned to join the first of a series of feasts in Brom and Mora's honor.

He glanced at the woman who would soon become the red-bearded warrior's life companion.

Mora, wearing a long silken gown, sat at Brom's side, while delicate-looking Astrah, her red hair flowing about her shoulders, was right beside Hogan. Through the thin material of her tunic and loose pants, he could feel the tantalizing heat of her flesh.

Brom looked uncomfortable in his ornately brocaded jacket and black silk pants. But as he had explained to Hogan on his arrival, Mora had chosen them. And he was still too unwell to argue with the strong-willed woman.

Mondlock was sitting a short distance away, dressed in one of the flowing robes that were part of his persona.

Laughter and good-natured teasing filled the large room. Uniformed officers joined with jewelry-adorned representatives of a dozen countries in the week-long series of parties that would end when the Kalabrian ruler and his consort stood before the Knower and a gathering of priests and shared their life pledges before the gods.

Two serving women carried tall vessels filled with honey-brew, the sweetened alcoholic beverage favored by the Kalabrians. Goblet after goblet was downed, especially by some of the younger army officers, and shouts for refills came regularly.

Brom had ignored the drink, and Hogan sipped his slowly while he thought of someone who was absent.

A flicker of sadness covered his face as he remembered another feast and the black-bearded wrestling champion of the army who had challenged him to a bout.

He had attended the delayed funeral rites and watched Brom light wood under the pallet bearing the body of his commander.

Brom, still looking wan from his illness, turned and studied Hogan. "You think of the wrestler, too?"

Hogan nodded. "He would have had some smart remark to make."

"I believe he is still making them. But in another place."

Hogan stayed silent, and the woman at his side squeezed his hand. Then she leaned over and whispered, "He is here, Hogan. At least his spirit is."

Hogan felt cheered by her warmth and affection.

"You're right," he admitted. "Zhuzak wouldn't miss a party if he could help it."

The serving of food had already started. A woman staggered into the large room carrying a huge platter of flatbakes. As she struggled around the room, the men helped themselves to the large circular breads. It was wonderfully suited for sopping up the rich gravies of meats.

Mora took several and handed them to Brom. Astrah followed her lead, giving one of the two flatbakes she had taken to Hogan, then hesitated before she allowed herself to nibble daintily on the other.

With the recent attempt on Brom's life in mind, Mora had taken no chances. Somebody could have slipped poison among the ingredients. She had insisted that portions of each dish be served to the hounds loitering outside the kitchen doors. Only after they seemed unharmed by the meals did she permit the women to serve the dishes to the guests.

Other women followed the first into the room, laden with huge trays piled high with meats and fish and a staggering variety of cooked vegetables.

Course after course came out of the kitchen piled, and as quickly as they appeared, they made the round and were emptied.

Mondlock had ignored most of the courses and selected the simple food he preferred. The clay bowl before him was filled with browned cereals, bits of vegetables and oil from the wild Kosan plant. No one had ever seen the wise man eat meat or fish or fowl.

A younger commander, filled with the courage of too much honeybrew, commented loudly on Mondlock's meal. "No teeth to eat the meal of a warrior, wise man?"

An older and wiser officer shook his head in disgust. "Be careful, Denko. The wise man has magic stronger than any warrior's teeth."

Stung by the rebuke, Denko pulled himself to his feet and staggered across the room, planting himself in front of Mondlock.

"Your magic has no teeth, old man. It didn't save commander Zhuzak or keep Peytok from trying to invade Kalabria," he cracked while he struggled to keep his balance.

Mondlock refused to return the officer's drunken stare. Instead, he concentrated on cleaning the last scraps of grain and vegetables from his bowl. Offended, Denko grabbed the clay bowl and threw it across the room.

Brom and Hogan started to get up, but the wise man gestured for them to remain seated.

Astrah bounded out of her seat and rushed over to pick up the bowl.

Mondlock signaled for her to bring it to him. After she did, Mondlock covered it with a napkin, then waved his hands over the concealed object.

He raised his head and calmly looked into the young officer's bloodshot eyes. The covered bowl began to rise into the air and move in measured pace toward the drunken soldier.

Frozen in place by a sudden fear, Denko watched the cover fall to the ground. The bowl that had been beneath had vanished.

In its place was a set of clay teeth. Floating in midair, the bridge began to snap as if it were in the mouth of some invisible being. Slowly Denko moved backward, trying to avoid the forward motion of the floating set of teeth, then tripped and fell face forward to the ground.

Suddenly the floating object sprang at him and clamped down hard on the left cheek of his behind. Screaming, the suddenly sober man tried in vain to tear the enchanted object from his body.

Brom glanced at Mondlock questioningly. The Knower seemed to have stopped breathing. His mouth was a rigid mask.

Then, as a response to Brom's look, he exhaled and let his features become soft again.

The floating set of teeth fell to the ground and shattered into bits of clay. As Denko jumped to his feet, everyone could see the two deep rows of teeth marks in his leather trousers.

Red-faced from humiliation, Denko rushed out of the tent as one of his companions shouted, "What say you about the magician's lack of teeth now?"

Laughter at his remark filled the air, and everyone returned to their meals. A loud, good-natured hubbub settled in the room, and the meal progressed to fruits and sweets.

Suddenly there was crashing of loud gongs, and a comely maiden wearing the uniform of the dance warriors stepped into the open circle in the middle of the room.

"The dance warriors will now perform in honor of their commander's wedding," she announced.

Astrah stole a glance at Mora. This would be the first time she had not joined the others in the dangerous acrobatic feats that demonstrated their skills.

Suddenly Mora made a decision. "And I will join with you," she said loudly, to the surprise of the guests.

Before Brom or Astrah could stop her, the tall lithe woman disappeared from the room.

"And I will dance with her," Astrah said, getting to her feet.

Black Jack knew better than to protest, and he said nothing as she strode from the room.

Brom leaned across to him. "There are times when silence is safer than discussion."

"Like now," Hogan replied, but he felt uneasy as he remembered how dangerous the dance warrior routines were. He leaned over to Brom.

"Can't you order them not to perform?"

"That would be like ordering the sun not to rise, the storm not to rage. If the women did agree to obey me, I am not certain I am willing to pay the devastating toll they would extract in revenge."

"What kind of revenge?"

"Think of the worst you can imagine."

"Astrah not going to bed with me."

Brom nodded wisely. "That, too."

So they waited for the performance, but when an hour had passed and the dance warriors still hadn't appeared, the guests became restless.

"Perhaps Mora has changed her mind," Hogan whispered to his table companion.

"Perhaps. But it would be the first time." Brom looked puzzled. "I wonder what's delaying them?"

His answer came when one of the dance warriors ran into the room, her clothing disheveled and her face covered with blood.

"Kidnappers have stolen the Lady Mora and her escort, Astrah!" she cried. "We tried to stop them, but there were too many."

Brom jumped to his feet, as did Hogan and the rest of the guests. The room was filled with loud, anxious questions and the quiet weeping of women.

"Who kidnapped them?"

"Hired soldiers, I think, Lord Brom. They were led by a pale man wearing the helmet of the Nordians."

Hogan and Brom exchanged looks. That sounded as though they were dealing with Peytok.

"There was somebody else with him who seemed to be in command. A tall man with yellow hair and odd, narrow eyes."

The two warriors knew him. The creature called Nis.

Brom bristled with anger as he turned to the heavy-set blond-bearded officer he had appointed to replace Zhuzak.

"Assemble five hundred of the finest of the Kalabrian troops, Captain Sondah. We leave immediately."

Hogan was already on his way outside when Brom stopped him. "Where are you going?"

"To get my equipment. I'll meet you outside."

He would have to put his joy on hold until he had helped settle the score against the creature who had caused so much suffering, and now stolen the woman dear to his heart.

He let out a whoop of anger and rage, and Brom stared after him, never having seen the usually calm Hogan in such a state.

23

While the Kalabrian troops gathered their weapons and armor, Hogan sorted through the equipment he brought with him.

As filled with rage as he was, he wanted to take everything with him, then realized that was impractical.

He made several trips to the stables with the weapons he had selected, then requisitioned a pair of heavy mounts to carry them and himself.

Black Jack opened the legs of the tripod on the .50-caliber M-60 machine gun and strapped it atop the saddle of one of the animals, then lashed two metal boxes containing belt-felt cartridges to the sides of the leather seat.

Improvising a pair of rifle holsters on the saddle of the second animal, he armed and shoved the M-16 with the grenade launcher into one of them, and a bulky zipper gun-case in the other. Then he loaded the saddle-bags with 40 mm incendiary and fragmentation grenades, as well as several dozen filled clips for his automatic rifle and Beretta.

As he was strapping the gun belt, complete with automatic pistol and his honed krall, around his waist, Brom came up to him.

Viewing the assortment of weaponry Black Jack was toting, Brom shook his head.

"These are strange fire-sticks," he commented.

Hogan handed him the other combination M-16 rifle and grenade launcher.

"This isn't going to be a battle of honor," Hogan muttered grimly. "Keep your sword in its scabbard and use this."

Fingering the weapon gingerly, Brom asked "What kind of fury does this fire-stick breathe?"

Black Jack explained how the combination weapon worked, then handed a quantity of clips to Brom and filled the launcher with fragmentation grenades.

The huge M-60 machine gun caught the Kalabrian's eye.

"That is a monstrous fire-stick," he said in awe.

Hogan knew that bringing the M-60 was overkill. The .50-caliber round could take out a car or chop through a thick brick wall. The 750-grain projectile was at least five times heavier than a standard .38 round and generated tremendous muzzle energy.

But he didn't care. Killing Zhuzak was bad enough. But kidnapping their women was too much. Now he was mad. Really mad.

"This time no more Mr. Nice Guy. There's going to be nobody alive when this is over except us."

One look at the expression on Hogan's face, and Brom believed him.

Captain Sondah rode up to announce that the troops were mounted and ready. Mondlock was riding beside the captain, wrapped in his long robe, his face solemn and determined.

"This is no place for a wise man," the Kalabrian warned.

"Only I know what the wizard who commands Peytok seeks," the Knower replied.

Brom was about to order Mondlock to stay behind when Black Jack interceded. "If everything else fails, I may have another way to get Mora and Astrah from the alien. But Mondlock will need to be there with us."

There was no time for Brom to ask for explanations. Already hours had passed since the women were kidnapped.

Mounting his horse, Brom turned to the new commander of the troops.

"Order the men to follow us," he snapped, then, with Hogan at his side, they began the journey.

THE SUN BEGAN to push the darkness from the sky, and still Brom and Hogan led an elite troop of five hundred Kalabrian warriors.

Rage and concern had kept fatigue at bay.

Brom permitted his men to rest their animals while he waited for the return of the scouts he had sent ahead to find the trail.

Soon they came riding back.

Their leader, a grizzled warrior named Juka, stopped his prancing animal before Brom.

"We found their trail. Unless they turn off before long, they are heading for the land that borders on the Forbidden Region."

Brom sounded puzzled. "What lies in the Forbidden Region that this creature craves so much that he continues to destroy innocents for it?"

Hogan turned to Mondlock. "You know, don't you?"

Mondlock nodded his head. "Or suspect."

"While the men water their animals, it's time we talked and came up with an alternative plan—as a last resort," Black Jack said bluntly to Brom.

"Are you suggesting we cannot rescue our women with our courage and weapons?"

"There's always that possibility," the American replied, then slid from his horse and waited for the other two to join him before he discussed his idea.

At first Mondlock refused to participate, then, after studying the concern in Brom's face, agreed to consider the plan if everything else failed.

PEYTOK KEPT PACING back and forth in the tent.

"You keep telling me to get ready for an attack by the Kalabrians.. How many are coming?"

"Many. More than you have faced before," Nis replied, wrapping his robe tightly around himself as he wearily lowered his body into a folding seat.

The nervous Nordian leader glanced at the two Kalabrian women sitting on the ground in a dark corner of the tent. They were bound and gagged to prevent them from crying out or attempting to escape.

Peytok seemed astonished. "All of them are coming here just to rescue two women?"

"Some of the creatures of this world are unpredictable," Nis replied.

The Nordian seemed confused by the reply. "Sometimes you sound like you were not one of those who inhabit this world, wizard."

Nis didn't answer. He wondered how Peytok would react if he knew how correct his assumption was.

"It is time for your men to find concealment from where they can ambush the Kalabrians," Nis suggested in a hard, commanding voice.

"Yes, yes," Peytok replied quickly. "I'll order it immediately."

Then he fled from the tent.

Nis forgot about the existence of the Nordian the moment he left the shelter. He lifted the cloth cover from an object lying on the floor near him. He studied the khaki-colored canister, and thought about Kalidonian.

Despite the number of canisters and shells Nis had gotten for him, the frantic old man had failed to carry out the plan.

For now he would have to concentrate his urgent search on this world.

He had considered using the gas-filled container on the Kalabrian palace and eliminating Brom. But Mondlock was there, too, and he needed the Knower to guide him to the source of the glowing stones.

He glanced at the two bound women who stared back at him with an unrelenting anger in their eyes. Then his gaze returned to the gas-filled canisters.

The women and this simple container would be the means through which he would finally find the source of the energy stones.

After that he could have no more need of these creatures.

24

The Kalabrian troops were approaching the highest part of the hilly country that bordered the Forbidden Region. High red-stone cliffs, carved by centuries of strong winds into strange shapes, rose around the riders on both sides of the wide packed-dirt road.

A perfect place for an ambush, Hogan thought as he surveyed the area from his lead horse. He moved his animal to Brom's side and pointed to the top of the cliffs ahead.

"One man with the right weapon could wipe out an army from up there," he said, "But first we would need to find the army."

As if in answer, three of the Kalabrian scouts came charging toward them from the direction of the Forbidden Region.

"Lord Brom, the Nordian forces are gathered in great numbers beyond the next pass in the hills," Juka reported hurriedly.

Brom was rubbing at his chin with restless energy. "It could work, Hogan," he muttered, "if we attack them, then retreat and lead them back here. What say you, Mondlock? Is the plan a good one?"

The Knower shrugged. "I am no expert in military matters. But I have seen greed and anger replace caution and logic."

"Then find a place from which you can safely view the forthcoming battle," Brom told him. "And you, Hogan, how much time do you need?"

"Ten minutes, if some of the warriors can give me a hand. Twenty if I do it alone."

Brom signaled three of his warriors to join them. "Follow Hogan's orders," he said crisply.

In a short while, the M-60 .50-caliber machine gun was anchored on top of the a cliff overlooking the plains. One of the cases of ammunition was open. The end of the twenty-five-foot belt of ammunition it contained was already fed into the bulky weapon.

Hogan dismissed the Kalabrians and began to load 40 mm grenades into the M-16 combo weapon, alternating incendiary and fragmentation types.

He stopped to check the view from his high perch. He could see clearly down the hills and across the wide sandy plains to the arid land where the Forbidden Region began.

He crawled to the edge of the rock and looked down at the road below, teeming with Kalabrian warriors.

"I'm ready," he shouted to the red-bearded leader, who waited on his high-strung, restless mount.

"Good," Brom shouted back. "I'll see you after the battle—or in hell."

"Whichever place we end up in," Hogan replied loudly.

Brom raised the howling sword he held in his right hand. Then he turned back to his men and shouted the command to attack.

"Death to the invaders. And eternal honor to brave warriors who fall in battle!"

PEYTOK HAD ALERTED the soldiers that the Kalabrians were about to attack. Nearly a thousand well-seasoned men, encased in armor and equipped with death-dealing weapons, waited for the enemy to begin their assault.

Those among them who had considered fleeing were forced to change their mind. The only way out was past the approaching troops, or across the vast desert to their rear.

And fire-breathing dragons and demons were rumored to dwell there.

Guzak, a brute of a man who was the troops elected captain, sat on his black horse at Peytok's side.

"Do we wait here or ride out to meet them?"

The Nordian clenched the reins he held tightly but didn't answer. He faced the man on his other side and looked at him questioningly.

"What say you, wizard?"

"Attack them first," came the order.

"Just have the gold ready to pay to us after the battle," Guzak warned. Then he trotted away and issued orders to his troops.

Nis and Peytok watched wave after wave of horsemen take off toward the hills in the distance.

"What will you do with the women after the battle?" Peytok asked. The Nordian had sneaked glances at the two female captives. Both were beautiful.

Nis knew what he wanted. "They can be your prize."

For the first time Peytok could hardly wait for the battle to begin.

HOGAN HAD WAITED for the troops to draw closer, then turned his attention to the zippered case. From inside he took out the Heckler & Koch PSG1 and opened its tripod legs.

Leaning down, he looked through the scope and moved the weapon around until he found what he was seeking.

Centered in his scope was the Nordian ruler, Peytok, and next to him stood Nis.

A cold wave of anger washed across the American as he rammed a fresh clip into the rifle and moved his finger to the trigger.

Carefully he adjusted the scope until the cross hairs centered on Peytok's chest.

A thousand yards separated him from his target. It was a long shot for the best of marksmen. But he thought of Astrah and Mora, and of Zhuzak, as he squeezed the trigger.

Through the scope Hogan saw Peytok suddenly press his hand against his chest as if he had felt a sudden pain, then pull it away and stare at the blood pouring into his hands.

He turned his head and focused his puzzled eyes on the wizard next to him.

Hogan could see his lips start to move, then stop as he fell forward.

Without taking time to taste the revenge, the American moved the weapon slightly to the right until the cross hairs were centered on the robed figure next to Peytok.

Through the scope Black Jack could make out the unconcerned expression on Nis's face.

Slowly the American started to pull the trigger again.

Then he allowed his finger to fall away from the trigger. Suddenly he understood what must be the reason for Nis's ability to vanish at will, and to be unharmed by bullets. It wasn't some sort of magic, at least not the old-fashioned kind. He was merely a projection—a three dimensional hologram—created by someone or something else.

Eliminating the figure who called itself Nis, even if it was possible to do it, would solve nothing.

But he had proposed an idea to Brom and Mondlock on how to make the real source of the threat come to them—and possibly a way to destroy it.

But below him the battle was already unfolding.

Unaware of the death of the ruler whose gold they were expecting, the soldiers charged the Kalabrians at the point where the road opened into the plains.

As they raced forward, they slashed with their axs, their knives, their spears and swords at empty air, demonstrating what they would do when they came into contact with the Kalabrians.

Brom's troops waited, seemingly unconcerned as the sea of armored bodies rushed on horseback or on foot toward them. Each was a trained, disciplined warrior, well armed with weapons and the knowledge that they were in the right.

At last the two forces clashed with the exploding sound of metal against metal, soon accompanied by shouts, screamed curses and the pitiful moans of the dying.

From above, the battleground appeared to heave with the mass of struggling men, and bright flashes of light glinted from weapons, only to be obscured by a crimson veil.

As Hogan has suggested, Brom had left his sword in its shoulder scabbard and was firing endlessly with the strange fire-stick his warrior blood brother had brought him. The empty clip was replaced by a full one time after time as the fire pellets chopped huge holes in the heads and bodies of the attacking enemy.

But even the loud sound of the angry fire-stick didn't frighten them away. They were used to fighting against strange weapons.

Brom was curious about the attachment to the fire-stick. As Hogan had instructed, he aimed the weapon at a group of horsemen charging toward him and pulled the trigger.

An oval metal egg flew in a graceful arc and fell amid the riders.

Suddenly a loud explosion seemed to tear open the miniature volcano of metallic bits that shredded the bodies of five mounted fighters. In terror the remaining four turned and fled in the direction of their camp.

Another launched egg missed its target and landed on the ground in front of a dozen mounted enemy.

The exploded metal shards tore into the forelocks of their animals. Wounded horses reared and threw their riders to the ground, then, in their panic to escape, trampled them.

Brom's troops continued to battle, man against man in a desperate bid for life. Attacker after attacker fell, and still they came on, drunk with blood lust.

All around him the enemy vied for a chance to deliver the killing blow to the red-bearded leader.

Brom stood his own, moving his horse quickly as he continued to fire his thundering weapon.

Finally he found himself too close to fire the death pellets. He slung the still-unfamiliar fire-stick on the horn of his saddle and withdrew his sword from its scabbard. Slashing to his left and right, he gutted a quartet who tried to tear him from his horse.

Another man charged from behind and swung a mace at Brom's head, narrowly missing contact.

Turning to face the new enemy, Brom raised the broadsword that had become his trademark.

With one powerful blow at the midsection of the mounted attacker, the heavy blade easily cleaved through metal and flesh and quickly separated the mercenary's head from his shoulders.

Suddenly, for no reason that was obvious, there was a lull in the fighting. Brom was used to such a phenomenon. Even the strongest of fighting men needed a brief respite.

Brom took advantage of the moment and surveyed the battlefield. More than half his force was still mounted. About the same number of the enemy were still able to fight.

The rest lay dead or dying.

There would be no rescue for the hired soldiers who could not walk. It was not the way of the ruthless men. They had no loyalty and left their seriously injured behind to their fate.

For those wounded Kalabrians who still lived after the battle, healers who had traveled with the troops would rush in to carry them from the field to tents where they could be treated.

Brom shielded his eyes and looked up at the cliffs.

He could see the partially hidden Hogan, who waited for his turn. It was time to move the site of the battle to another location.

Brom whipped his broadsword in the air over his head until it made a penetrating howling sound.

Kalabrians and Peytok's men turned toward the source of the loud mourning noise. Then the Kalabrians, recognizing the signal to pull back, began an orderly retreat.

The hired soldiers let out a loud cheer, but their elected commander, Guzak, rode his horse among them, screaming in rage.

"What are you cheering about? The Kalabrian leader is escaping." Then he reminded them, "There's a reward of gold for the man who kills him!"

Suddenly, as Hogan had predicted, the soldiers regrouped and charged after the retreating troops.

HOGAN WAITED for the Kalabrians to race past him before he opened fire with the machine gun.

Round after round tore into the pursuers. Still they came, rushing wildly into the storm of lead from above that tore them into shattered corpses.

Looking up, Guzak waved his short sword in rage at the man he saw crouched behind the strange spitting weapon.

He turned to a group of archers. "Kill him," he ordered.

Six archers raised their powerful bows and loosened a wave of feathered death toward the cliff.

Hogan flattened himself and felt the arrows whizz overhead. Then he resumed his position and began his assault again.

A sustained burst of fire churned blood and tissue out of the chests of four archers. The remaining two panicked. They turned and bolted toward their camp.

Guzak bellowed at them in frustration. "Come back, cowards!"

He stopped yelling forever when fire from Hogan's .50-caliber deathmaker exploded his head as he catapulted from his horse.

The Kalabrians wheeled their horses about to face the remaining pursuers. Brandishing their weapons, Brom and his men charged back with fierce grins on their faces.

The sounds of savage fighting echoed through the hills as Kalabrian warriors avenged the men, women and children the enemy soldiers had murdered in their lust for treasure.

One by one they slaughtered the enemy until the handful left who were not wounded ran in terror from the site of destruction.

WHILE HIS MEN RESTED, Brom let the healers onto the battle scene to deal with the wounded and the dead.

Then he stood and watched as Hogan climbed down from his high perch.

"You are well?"

Hogan waited until he was at Brom's side before he answered. "Not a scratch. How about you?"

Brom grunted his reply. "I am still whole."

Hogan scanned his face and body, covered with blood and sweat. "You need a bath."

The Kalabrian grinned proudly. "After I present myself to the gods."

"But before the wedding, I hope."

Brom looked startled, as if Hogan had reminded of something important. "Mora and Astrah are still captives. Peytok may want to avenge the death of his mercenaries."

"Not unless he finds a way to do it from hell," Hogan replied.

"He is dead?"

"He better be," Black Jack said, "or I'm going to ask for a refund from the company that made the gun."

Brom slapped Hogan on the back. "Then it's time we retrieved our women."

He signaled one of his men to bring a horse for Hogan. "Let him who harms my chosen mate tremble!" Brom bellowed. He was taking a public oath. "He will not live, or I am not Brom, Lord of Kalabria!"

25

Riding ahead of the warriors, Brom and Hogan descended into the plains and moved toward the cluster of tents in the distance.

Mondlock rode beside them, silent and contemplative.

Beyond the encampment was the start of the Forbidden Region.

Brom signaled for Captain Sondah to join them. "Have the men spread out and search the area for any of Peytok's men who may still live."

While Captain Sondah and the troops began their careful search, Hogan and Brom continued their journey to the cluster of tents.

Mondlock the Knower now rode behind them as the Kalabrian ruler had ordered.

Someplace in the camp, the two warriors knew, were Mora and Astrah. They were close enough to see the colorful tents, all blues and yellows and reds. They stopped on the camp's perimeter and waited.

The man called Nis stepped out of a tent and faced them. In his hands he held a khaki-colored can.

The three mounted men recognized it immediately. Such an object had contained the substance that had killed the villagers.

"You are without an army," Brom warned.

"I don't need anything if I have this," Nis replied, moving a finger to the release mechanism.

"If we die, you die," Brom shouted.

Hogan whispered in his ear. "No, he doesn't. He isn't real."

Brom looked puzzled, then skeptical. "He is here."

"I'll explain later. Just believe me. He is like an image conjured up by a magician."

"My understanding fails," the Kalabrian muttered.

"Mine too. But I have an idea how it's done." Hogan looked at Mondlock. "Do you?"

Slowly Mondlock lifted his hand into the air as if to ward off evil. "More than I did before."

Nis thought the talking had gone on long enough and became impatient. "Tell me the source of the glowing rocks that were in your pendants," he demanded.

The three from Kalabria stared at him. He looked pale and tired.

Black Jack turned to the Knower. "It's up to you. You're the only one who knows."

"If we give it to him, what guarantee do we have he will leave our world forever?"

"Once I find the source, I will have no need to return here," Nis promised.

The American ignored Nis's reply.

"We don't have any real guarantees. But there's always the chance that he means it. And if we don't, we're done anyway."

The elderly wise man became silent and closed his eyes, then announced his decision. "Release the women. Allow them and the men to return to Tella, and I will lead you to the source."

"No. I will release you all *after* you lead me to it."

Mondlock turned and stared into the sky. His lips were moving but no sound came from them.

Hogan wondered if he was praying.

Finally the Knower faced Nis again.

"I will lead you to the temple of Ost. It is not far from here. But before you enter it, you must release all of us."

"Agreed."

Mondlock looked at Hogan coldly. The unspoken message in his eyes was "If your plan doesn't work, our world is dead."

ASTRAH AND MORA, their gags and ropes removed, rode with Hogan and Brom across the Forbidden Region. But the other warriors had been ordered to stay behind.

Ahead of them rode the creature who called himself Nis and Mondlock the Knower.

Except for Nis, the travelers wore head coverings to shield them from the unyielding sun.

Hogan had explained the situation to the women after they wondered why their men hadn't killed their captor.

"Ost will punish us," Astrah warned her man.

"Unless we do this, there won't be anyone to punish," Black Jack replied. Even Mora had no answer to that.

The journey took almost half a day, and it was difficult riding.

The Forbidden Region wasn't a flat stretch of sand. Hills and gullies were everywhere, as were ravines and canyons.

The sun had baked the area into a lifeless zone, and water was scarce, so they only moistened their lips from their canteens.

When they were approaching a place crisscrossed with crevices and ravines, Mondlock raised his hand to signal a halt.

"We walk from here," he called out, dismounting from his horse.

Brom and the women followed him. Hogan paused for a moment to load some grenades into his combo weapon, then moved quickly to catch up with them.

Mondlock led the way down a path, then into a narrow ravine that was barely wide enough to let a person pass.

Finally he came to a large flat rock. Waiting until the others caught up with him, he pressed his hand against the stone and waited.

A muffled sound echoed from behind the rocky wall. Then the large rock began to move slowly inward, swinging open on hidden hinges built into the rock frame more than a thousand years ago.

A strange glow filled the entrance.

Mondlock reached inside and pulled out a large heavy robe that seemed to weigh as much as he did.

He turned to the two warriors and their women.

"Wait out here," he ordered, then covered himself from his head to his feet with the robe and led Nis inside.

The glow seemed to be coming from some inner chamber. Mondlock knew the way. As a priest of Ost, he had been there many times.

"Where are the glowing rocks?" Nis demanded.

"Be patient. They are here," the Knower replied softly.

He led Nis to another stone door. He ran his fingers over a series of carved symbols before he pressed on a section of the door.

Noiselessly it swung open.

Inside the small room was a massive statue made of some heavy metal. The huge figure was holding a giant covered bowl in its hands.

"Inside the bowl are the rocks you seek," Mondlock said sadly.

Nis's eyes glowed. It was obvious he could feel the energy. Quickly he started to advance toward the statue, ignoring the presence of the wise man.

Mondlock left the room rapidly, then pressed his hand against the door, which swung closed.

He raced out of the temple, pausing only to seal the outer door, then gestured for the others to follow him.

Brom looked at him. "What happened?"

"There is no time to explain now. We need to leave this place."

They made their way out of the ravine, then after the women were mounted, the three men sprang into the saddles.

Without looking back, they raced back across the desert toward the camp where the warriors waited.

INSIDE THE TEMPLE, Nis removed the cover of the statue's vessel and stared in astonishment at the vast number of glowing rocks inside.

There was enough here to sustain the Guardian for more years than most of the creatures on this planet would live.

Nis's real substance, the small dark shadow that had followed on his heels into the temple, could feel the outpouring energy. It was strengthening him.

The shadow began to grow and take form. A large egg-shaped form. Rapidly the egglike shell expanded as the energy continued to saturate it.

Like a creature who had been starved too long, the Guardian couldn't get enough of the energy. It was again becoming the powerful force it had once been before the supplies of energy rocks had vanished.

Soon worlds would submit to its rule. Soon the glory that once was would be again. And, through him, the Guardians would again rule.

His outer shell began to crowd against the walls of the small temple room. It was time to stop absorbing.

Once he had exterminated the inhabitants of this world, he could return whenever he needed to be renewed.

The Guardian turned to leave. Then he saw the sealed door.

He tried to break it with his power. Massive energy was launched against the barricade, but it held firm.

He could sense why. Under the stone exterior the door was made of an insulating metal resistant to the strength of the glowing rocks.

There was something else he could do. Cover the vessel and stop the flow of energy.

He searched for the metal lid. Then he realized it was under him. There was no way to reach it.

Meanwhile the emissions from the vessel continued to pour into him. And he kept expanding, getting larger and larger.

MONDLOCK GAZED UP at the position of the sun in the sky, then pulled his horse to a halt.

"Dismount," he ordered.

Quickly scanning the area, he found the opening in the rocks he sought.

"In here," he shouted, and led the way inside.

Fumbling his way, he led the others deep into the crevice.

They were in a cavern. The sounds of dripping water echoed as they entered a large chamber deep in the belly of the planet.

Even in the darkness they could feel the presence of icicle-shaped stalactites hanging from the ceiling.

Astrah gasped as she bumped into something.

Hogan moved quickly to her side, Beretta in hand.

Then he felt the cone-shaped object. It was a stalagmite.

"Just formations from the minerals in the cave," he explained. He knew something about them from a visit he had made to the Carlsbad Caverns as a teenager.

Suddenly there was a deep, muffled roar, and the ground shook violently, causing several of the stalactites to crash down.

Brom grabbed for his sword as he demanded, "What was that noise?"

Hogan had heard it before. He couldn't remember where, but it was not in this world.

Then it came to him. A test he had witnessed of a nuclear device in the Nevada desert.

He started worrying about the possibility of radiation.

"The creature is gone," Mondlock said quietly.

Mora was skeptical. She turned to Hogan. "You said he couldn't be killed."

"I'll let Mondlock explain it," Black Jack replied, still thinking about the possible fallout.

Mondlock's answer was slow to come as he gathered his thoughts. "Hogan had suggested that whoever controlled the figure called Nis had probably been starved for his peculiar form of nutrition for a very long time." He paused and thought about his last words. "Yes, a very long time, I suspect. If the creature behaved like hungry humans do, he wouldn't stop consuming what he sought until he destroyed himself by overeating."

"What happens to Ost?" Astrah asked worriedly.

"He was there in the beginning, and he will always be with us as long as this world exists," Mondlock replied in a reverent tone.

"When can we leave this place?" Brom demanded.

"Now. The temple was built to contain such an event. All of it is lined with a material that absorbs the harm. It has been passed down in secret ancient writing that had originated from Ost himself. It is safe."

"Are you sure?" Hogan questioned.

"There is recorded in the annals of the temple a similar explosion centuries ago. We had to protect ourselves from the shaking of the ground, but now the evil emanations have been negated by Ost's preparations at the dawn of time."

"Then let's get out of here and go home," Black Jack said, sounding relieved.

EPILOGUE

Hiram Wilson was very concerned. There had been no word from Hogan for more than a week, and the President still was waiting for the detailed report.

He decided to face the wrath of the man in the Oval Office.

When the arrangements had been made, and he was finally led into the office, the tall man behind the desk looked up at his Intelligence aide.

"My secretary said you have something that couldn't wait, Hiram."

"It's about that report, sir."

The President waved a handful of letters at him. "See these? Do you know what they are?"

"No, sir," Wilson replied nervously.

"They're letters of congratulations from the governments of fifty countries. Some of them not our friends. They're all delighted with the fact that we took decisive action before the terrorists could use the stolen gas."

The President stared at the stack of mail on his desk. "It's going to take me a whole week to answer them," he said. Then he thought of something else and looked up at his aide.

"Tell Black Jack congratulations for me."

HOGAN WASN'T anyplace where Wilson could reach him, and for that he was grateful. In fact, he toyed with the idea of not leaving the room dressed in the ridiculous clothes he'd been given.

"You look wonderful," the soft female voice said with admiration.

It was Astrah, wearing a long, flowing blue garment topped with a short silken cape. Her long, strawberry-colored hair was twisted into a braid that hung down her neck.

"I look ridiculous," Hogan growled as he glanced at himself in the mirror.

Mora and Astrah had selected a brocaded white shirt for him to wear over a pair of short, wide, brocaded pants. Matching brocaded slippers covered his large feet.

He felt like a clown. Embarrassed, he asked, "Who dresses like this?"

"The man who stands beside the groom. It is tradition."

"What does the groom wear?"

His question was answered when the door opened and Brom strode in.

His apparel was similar to Hogan's except that his shirt, pants and slippers were made of black silk heavily embroidered with gold.

He cast a piercing glance at Hogan. "How do I look?" Then he added, "Don't tell me the truth unless you are in the mood to duel."

"You both look wonderful," Astrah replied. "And so does Mora, as you will soon see."

Brom squirmed in his ceremonial clothing. "Do you realize that in less than an hour I will be a married man?"

They could hear music starting to play in the distance.

"I do now," Black Jack replied.

"And you are going to let me go through with the ceremony?"

Hogan grinned. "I don't think a thousand warriors could stop you," he replied with a knowing wink.

The red-bearded giant grunted and walked out of Hogan's room.

"It's time for us to go, too," Astrah announced.

Hogan avoided looking at himself again in the mirror. "I suppose I can suffer in these things for a day," he muttered.

"Until the time comes for you to wear the golden clothes of the groom," she replied, then tucked her arm under his and led him into the corridor.

Suddenly Hogan thought of Hiram Wilson. There must be another mission coming up for which he was needed.

He would have to return to his own world soon.

Glancing at the glowing girl who clung to him and let undisguised affection fill her eyes, Hogan began to soften.

Maybe not.

He'd think about it again in a few days.

Go for a hair-raising ride in

JAMES AXLER

DEATH LANDS®

Dark Carnival

Trapped in an evil baron's playground, the rides are downhill and dangerous for Ryan Cawdor and his roving band of warrior-survivalists.

For one brief moment after their narrow escape, Ryan thinks they have found the peace and idyll they so desperately seek. But a dying messenger delivers a dark message....

Available in January at your favorite retail outlet, or order your copy now by sending your name, address, zip or postal code along with a check or money order for $4.99 plus 75¢ postage and handling ($1.00 in Canada), payable to Gold Eagle Books to:

In the U.S.	In Canada
Gold Eagle Books	Gold Eagle Books
3010 Walden Avenue	P.O. Box 609
P.O. Box 1325	Fort Erie, Ontario
Buffalo, NY 14269-1325	L2A 5X3

Please specify book title with your order.
Canadian residents add applicable federal and provincial taxes.

DL14R